9/21

Peep Show

Also by Joshua Braff

The Unthinkable Thoughts of Jacob Green

A NOVEL BY

JOSHUA BRAFF

Algonquin Books of Chapel Hill 2010

Published by
ALGONQUIN BOOKS OF CHAPEL HILL
Post Office Box 2225
Chapel Hill, North Carolina 27515-2225

a division of
WORKMAN PUBLISHING
225 Varick Street
New York, New York 10014

Printed in the United States of America.
Published simultaneously in Canada by Thomas Allen & Son Limited.
Design by Anne Winslow.

Photograph credits: chapter 4, PhotofestNY; chapter 10, PhotofestNY; chapter 14, Superstock Inc.—Getty Images; chapter 15, Jerry Berndt—Getty Images; chapter 18, Andreas Schlegel—Getty Images; chapter 19, Julian Wasser—Getty Images; all other photographs courtesy of the author.

LIBRARY OF CONGRESS CATALOGING-IN-PUBLICATION DATA
Braff, Joshua, [date]
Peep show : a novel / by Joshua Braff.—1st ed.
p. cm.
ISBN 978-1-56512-508-7
1. Teenage boys—Fiction. 2. Fathers and sons—Fiction.
3. Jewish families—Fiction. 4. Vocational guidance—Fiction.
5. Pornography—Fiction. 6. Jewish fiction. I. Title.
PS3602.R344P44 2010
813'.6—dc22 2009051631

10 9 8 7 6 5 4 3 2 1
First Edition

Jill

Part I

Spring 1975

David

I KNOW I'M IN HERE. Sleeping but not really. A movie with extras, so vivid and involved. I'm in my father's theater in the dream, a room off the lobby. Two dancers want their picture taken, arm in arm. I lift a camera from the floor but it's heavy and has a sash strap that tangles. They laugh as I struggle and when I see them through the lens they both have their tops off. I try to shoot but there's no click, no sound or flash. The girls are annoyed and restless and one of them points at me.

"You need to lift it from the back. From the *back*!" I watch them approach me and one of them kneels on the floor at my feet. I hear a crash, a heavy thudding or a tumbling of great weight and glass that's smashing downward outside my door and I am sitting up before I think to do so.

I run to the hallway. My mother and sister are both staring down the staircase. Debra looks at me.

"It slipped," she says.

"What slipped?"

"The TV," she says. "It was heavy."

I walk closer to them and look over the banister. It's my dad's. Upside down on the landing with the screen smashed, a brick to a windshield. There are four crude puncture holes in the wall, which curves around the circular staircase. Two of the pegs in the railing are gone. My mother's goal was to move it while I slept, to bury it in the garage with all the hefty bags and boxes marked SECULAR. Nice job. It is so rare that Miss Hasid USA is the idiot, the one to blame. I feel vindicated standing here next to my sister, so I laugh a little but it's not meant to be mean. My mother stares at me, pondering how to distribute this mess to someone other than herself. Instead, she heads for her room.

"Why throw it down, Ma?" I say.

"We didn't throw it," says Debra.

"You didn't? Look at it."

My mother reverses and walks quickly toward me. "Today is the most important day of my life. If you want me to feel bad just . . . *don't*."

"I was sleeping. All I asked is—"

"Okay, David?"

"Why it was tossed down."

"It slipped," says Debra.

My mother heads to her room but stops again. "I have twenty-five people coming here in a half hour. Let me tell you what I need from you. There is a poster over your bed of a man wearing lipstick. I need you to take it down. Please go do it now."

We stare at each other. I turn to face what she sees. A portrait of Ziggy Stardust bending over a microphone stand. When I look back at her she is already in her room.

"Look at the holes in the wall," Debra says softly, still on the staircase.

"Get dressed!" my mother says. "He'll be here in fifteen minutes."

"You said a half hour," Debra says.

"Just hurry."

I follow my sister into her room and stand by her dresser. "That belonged to Dad."

"It was an accident," she says. "Leave her alone."

"It didn't roll down, Deb."

"You really think she'd do that on purpose?"

"To him, yes."

"On *this* day, of all days? Let me get dressed. The rabbi's coming."

"Maybe *he* can fix the wall."

My sister doesn't laugh. She doesn't even smile. She looks frazzled, searching for a hairbrush, the dress she'll wear. I sit on her bed and look up at her light yellow walls. Three portraits of the grand rabbi, blessed be he, hang in this bedroom. By the window he's got the beard of Santa Claus and he's trying to smile. A melancholy grin. The bags under his eyes look like twenty-pound teardrops. Maybe they're filled with two thousand years of oppression and pogroms. Sean Cassidy, a *Teen Beat* poster, hung there just two years ago. Parker Stevenson was above the bed and Leif Garrett and that kid from *James at Fifteen* were on the closet door. She had a stuffed Big Bird that used to sit on the bed and an *H.R. Pufnstuf* doll that played the theme song when you pulled the string. They're all gone now. Bagged and tagged and piled into the garage. I watch her lay out her dress, black, long sleeved, and nearly to the floor.

"Did you do the prayer?" my mother yells from her room.

"I'm trying!" my sister says, looking at me.

"I saw Dad the other night," I tell her.

She freezes then. "In New York?"

"He said he might drop by. To congratulate you."

"Here?"

"Yes."

"Tonight?"

"That's what he said but—"

"Does Mom know?"

I stand from her bed and make my way to the door. "I thought I'd let you tell her."

"Dena!" my mother yells, which is what she now calls Debra. My sister reaches under her bedside table and slides a pitcher of water and a basin out into view. She pours the water over her right hand and then over the left. She repeats this three times and says a blessing in Hebrew under her breath. When she finishes she dries her hands and glances my way.

"Let me get dressed."

"Are you ready for this?" I say.

She pushes the pitcher underneath the table. "You asked me that last night."

"I forget what you said."

She shrugs and looks down at her fingernails. "It's not a funeral, you know?"

"It isn't?"

"No."

"Feels like it. Like someone's about to get buried."

"You mean me?" she says, and her eyes meet mine.

Maybe I do. Maybe that's what it is. I look at my sister and it feels like she's leaving. As if I need to miss her. Before our father moved to New York, we'd sit on the top step of the staircase together and listen to the parties, the people he'd bring home from work. They were loud and they'd cackle as they drank and I remember laughing on purpose so Debra wouldn't be scared.

"Why are you staring at me?" she says.

"Am I?"

"David," my mother says from the hall, and I wait for her to say more.

"Mom called you," Debra says.

I nod and head back into the hallway, then into my room. I don't see her. I lift my Instamatic from the bedside table and take a picture of the wreckage on the stairs. The disfigured wall. *Click*. The snapped railing. *Click*. The TV is wrapped in its own cord and there's broken glass beneath it. *Click*. The second I return to my bedroom I see what's missing. Un-fucking-believable. I find her in the garage, in one of her potato-sack dresses, rolling up Bowie as quickly as she can.

"Give it back to me."

"Just for the ceremony."

"It belongs to me, Ma!"

"I'll give it back to you tonight."

"It's mine!"

She hands it to me. "Then keep your door closed."

"I said I would."

"And help me with the television."

"Is that a joke?"

"No."

"Oh, you need a favor . . . from me. Just bend your knees and pick it up," I say, and start to walk inside.

"Please!"

I run past her and into the house. I grab the TV from the sides, hoist it onto my shoulder.

"Be careful of the glass," she yells, and I'm flying with it through the living room and into the kitchen, the laundry room, and out to the garage, where I get some momentum, and fling the thing into a silent arc that just *exploooodes* when it hits the concrete floor. The screen turns to dust and the pieces scatter everywhere and slide in shards within seconds. My mother's face is all I see from the laundry room. It's the one I'd expect she'd have. "Great," she says, softly, shutting the door.

I shouldn't have done that. The idea swirled in my mind and it felt like it would be satisfying but it broke into bits instead of just landing in a chunk. It'll take days for her to get over it. But of course she wants me to let her down. I'm the dissident, just giving her what she expects. I pick up a piece of the carnage, a hunk of cabinet, and throw it like a Frisbee at the pyramid of boxes. It sticks in one marked BOOKS AND PICS before dropping to the floor. I walk over to the box and tear it open. *Disenfranchised Grief; Trapped inside the Mirror; The Picture of Dorian Gray; Goodbye, Columbus; Sunshine; Mr. and Mrs. Bo Jo Jones*. The photographs and postcards are stacked in yellow folders. Some of them are pinned to each other, from water I guess, and some completely ruined. Sunsets, lots of them, Long Beach Island . . .

"David!" my mother yells from inside.

My parents in white cable-knit sweaters. Her head is tilted, almost touching his shoulder. He has the cigar. Another one of my dad, a thin mustache, waving from the driver's seat of a Cadillac. Debra as a baby. Some lady on the couch. An orange tree. Our neighbor Mrs. Shapiro with Heather Ewing. Me and Heather Ewing on the driveway. A couple of years ago, in the tenth grade, she showed me and Bobby Finkelstein her vagina. We never asked her to. She just volunteered. I remember it being hairy and forbidden and Bobby reached to touch it and Heather punched his ear and it bled. Here's a picture of Heather, Debra, and my dad. He's probably fifteen years younger than he is now—no goatee or double chin—and he's blowing into the tip of his thumb like a bugler, his cheeks filled with air. I open another box right next to it. Record albums and books on top of more pictures. *Brain Salad Surgery, Rubber Soul, Live from Folsom Prison. Violence in America. Business and Finance. Hitler's Lair. Helmut Newton.* On the cover of the Helmut Newton is a woman on her knees on the floor with a horse-riding bit in her mouth. Her nipples have paint on them but it might be food, like smeared blueberries.

"He's here," my mother screams. "He's *here,* Dena!"

Through the small garage-door window I see him. A holy man from Brooklyn. Tiny and slump shouldered in an oversized fedora. I remember him from the *baal teshuva* compound in Maine. Rabbi Liebersohn. He has a long white beard that ends above the paunch in his stomach and kind wrinkled eyes. He glances down at the wet grass below his shoes and lifts his foot. Two young men, in the same black clothes and hat, are at his side. They hold his elbows, moving him slowly toward our porch, as if he might slip from their hands. When my mother comes out to greet him, she smiles and sort of bows, her fingers clasped behind her back. He says something and then cranes his neck from one end of the house to the other.

I grab as many pictures as I can from both boxes and run inside and up to my room. I spill them on the carpet, separating the good from the destroyed. My father in a top hat looks like the character from Monopoly. My mother and sister on a sled on a hilltop. My mother, smiling in this one, the way she just smiled at the holy man. I hear a baby scream downstairs, then a woman's voice in Yiddish. When I open my door I see them. The Levitzes, the Sandbergs, the Hymans—all synagogue people she met at the compound—plus the Tartaskys and the Greenbaums, the Mitklins and Debra's new best friend, Sarah, wearing the same exact black dress as all the girls. The married women wear *sheitels*, which are bad brown wigs, and the men have long beards and yarmulkes or hats. Big families arrive together but separate into different sides of the *mechitzah*, a dividing wall for those with penises and those without. The Levitzes are typical with their five or six kids. A rising slope of heads, the oldest a teen. Their mother, Chaya, is the missionary. She got my mom to turn *frum*. I remember because I'd just had my ninth birthday, Debra was seven, and my mom lost a baby, a miscarriage. It was October 1967. Chaya was always with Becca when they came to the house. These ladies in wigs in our kitchen, talking to my mother in whispers. My father was there and I knew he wasn't happy. He especially despised the records they gave my mom, the sermons she played all day long. The grand rabbi in his early thirties. Deb and I knew every beat of them, every word, the rising applause, the funny curls in his accent. But we never knew how far it would go. The level she'd take it. Becca's husband, a man named Pinchus, is a "learner," a guy who studies Torah all day and night. He's the man who introduced her to Yiddish and Talmud and the Shulchan Aruch. I see him talking to his wife right now. She's the head of the "snoods" as I call them, my mother's new clique. Debra says they keep lists of who did and didn't do what in the remarkably stringent and uneventful world of Hasidic Judaism. So-and-so was seen touching the hand of a yeshiva boy on Gilman Street at 5:50 p.m. Blah-blah was seen eating a Snickers bar behind the synagogue and Dumb Fuck didn't wear a yarmulke in the presence of a rabbi.

From my perch on the top step I see the holy man lifting his arms, trying to get everyone's attention. I run to my closet and see my black suit and my blue suit. I put on the blue and walk down into the growing crowd. My sister is on the other side of the dividing wall, surrounded by snoods. I wave to her through the openings in the screen, but she doesn't see me. Some of the women remain kind to me, in a surface way, and smile even though they know I'm never becoming one of them. The men are less understanding, especially those who tried to convert me at the compound in Maine. Like Avraham Neidelman, I see him right now. He said he wanted us to become "brothers" and bought me a gold-plated prayer book, which he inscribed. I forget what it said exactly but the words *brothers, Talmud,* and *final redemption* were all there, written in calligraphy. When I told him I'd talked to my father and had decided to stop going to Maine, he sent me a postcard with the grand rabbi's face on it. He wrote, "God does not watch over those who ignore the Torah. Call me." Now I'm standing here on the male side of the *mechitzah* with him, a dot of blue in a sea of beards and black. When my eyes meet his and others, they look away, signaling I've betrayed them. A man I've never seen before yells, "*Shush, nu, nu!*" and the room goes quiet quickly. I see my mother atop the stairs. We stare at each other for a moment and she descends as if entering a play. The holy man begins in a Yiddish accent, facing only the men.

"No matter how far an individual has distanced himself from God by his previous behavior, it is possible, always possible, for him to return, depending on his effort, all the way to great and meaningful closeness with his Creator. Rabbi Yochanan said, 'Great is *teshuvah,* repentance, for it causes a person's verdict to be torn up.' And Rabbi Yehudah said, 'One who has the opportunity to do the same sin and, this time, does *not* do it—he is a *baal teshuva,* a master of repentance.'

"*Baruch Ata Adonai,*" he says, and all the men join in. "*Elohenu Melech Ha-olam, Shehekianu V'Kimanu V'Higianu, Lizman Hazeh.*"

Through the squares of the *mechitzah*, I watch Becca place a brown wig on my mother's head. It sits high and boxy so she tugs at it, though it keeps popping up. My mother might be crying—she's covered her eyes with both hands—but I guess it's out of happiness. The holy man says two more prayers and it's official. The two of them are now *BT*s as they're called; *baalai teshuva* in Hebrew. Converts from nonobservant Jews to Hasids in just under three and a half years. When I get close to my mom I am unsure if I should kiss her in front of these people. She reaches to touch my shoulder but then presses her cheek against mine. I am surprised to feel her face. I put my arms around her and she pats my back.

"The happiest I've ever been," she says, and I try not to glance at the misshapen wig.

"Then I'm happy for you."

My sister walks up behind her. They squeeze each other and rock back and forth.

"I love you," my mother says, and now really begins to weep. "I love you. I love you."

IN THE BACK of my parents' wedding album is a picture of my father. He's sitting at a table marked 9 with an enormous bouquet of autumn flowers in the middle. There's a cigar in his hand and he's talking to my mother's brother, Don, a man who died before I was born. In my uncle's face I recognize my mother's eyes and nose and chin. It makes me sad for her. A sibling. To lose him so young. I see headlights out my window, a car pulling into the driveway. My father. I run downstairs. Debra and my mother are washing dishes.

"Guess who's here?" I say as he lets himself in through the laundry room door.

"*Mazel tov!*" he yells, and lifts a bag of wrapped gifts above his head. Debra plucks off her rubber gloves and walks to him.

"Get over here, little girl," he says, and lifts her before kissing her eye socket a thousand times.

"Enough!" my mother says, yanking Debra's nightgown back over her legs.

"I missed you," he says. "I missed my baby girl."

"Martin," my mother says.

"What?"

"You didn't call."

"A wig?" he says. "You're wearing a wig?"

She touches it and looks at the floor.

"When did you get a—?"

"Don't."

"Don't what, Mick?"

"Don't be unkind."

He turns to me and blinks, working to form a smile. "Why would I do that? I'm crazy about you, aren't I?"

My mother looks at her husband, fifteen years her senior. He leans in to kiss her on the cheek.

"You should've called first."

"I knew today was the big one. I didn't want to bother you. It was today, right?"

My mother heads for the hallway. "They have school in the morning, Martin. Please don't stay too long."

"I don't want to drive back to the city now."

The sound comes from her nose. She shakes her head all the way to the stairs.

"Wait, Mick. I got you something, a gift."

"No, thank you."

"For the occasion, wait."

"No, thank you," she says from the hallway. We hear her door slam.

"She's angry with me. The Hasid is angry with me."

"Where have you been?" says Debra, and my father laughs.

"What do you mean where have I been? Where have *you* been?"

"I'm here, Daddy. I'm always here."

"I'm here too, so don't worry about what was and what wasn't. Open up your gifts."

Debra gets a snow globe with the Empire State Building inside and a porcelain China doll in a green shiny dress. I get a book called *Earth's Filthiest Jokes* and a brand new camera by Nikon. It's beautiful, the SL2, the newest model, and it's hard to believe he bought it and I'm holding it, so heavy in my hand.

"You're a photographer, aren't you?" he says.

"Thank you."

My father takes his jacket off and yawns with his mouth wide. He tells us he's pooped and asks if he can sleep in Debra's room. She nods and smiles and shakes the snow globe. "So where've you been?" she says in a younger voice than her own.

He points at the doll. "Do you like it or not?"

"Of course I do."

"Good then. I'm happy. Anybody got a toothbrush?"

• • •

DEBRA WATCHES HIM brush his teeth in the reflection of the bathroom mirror. She follows him into her room and pulls out the trundle bed beneath her mattress. I see them lying together on their sides but cannot hear what they're saying. When I walk in he asks if I like the joke book and if I'd read "the one about the bull balls." I grab the filthy joke book and open it to a random page. The one I find to read aloud is about a rooster that gets syphilis in Tijuana. I watch my dad laugh with his mouth wide, as he wipes the deep creases near his eyes. He was forty when I was born in 1958. My mom is forty-two now, eighteen when she met him. They separated more than five times between Debra's birth and now and neither of us knows if their marriage is officially over or not. Only married women wear *sheitels,* so at least for today they're married.

I tell him I found boxes of old pictures in the garage and he sits up and asks to see them. From my room I get the one of him waving from the Cadillac. "A 1964 Caddy," he says.

I kiss my sister on the cheek and reach to touch my father's arm. "I'm going to sleep," I tell him.

He pulls me toward him for a hug and whispers in my ear. "Tomorrow. Come to work with me. Bring the camera."

I nod, knowing I can't go, and leave the room.

My father screams, "*Mickey!* How come you won't open my gift? I got ya something nice. Just come see it. I think you'll like it."

"Stop that!" she says from her doorway. "*Shhhhh.* They have school in the morning."

....

"Okay, then just talk to me for a sec."

"I'm tired," she says.

"It took a long time but you . . . finally got what you wanted, huh? The whole Megilla, right, Mick?"

"My name is Miriam," she says. She turns out the hall light and everything is dark. "They have school in the morning, Martin. Let her sleep."

"But I got an announcement. A bedtime announcement, for my family. *David!*"

"Yes?" I call.

"Come back."

He's on his feet when I get there, moving toward the doorway.

"I dumped my old apartment. The small one, it wasn't big enough. My new place is perfect and I'm ready to have my kids come and see me."

"Where is it?" Debra says.

"In the city."

"Where was the last one?" Debra says.

"It doesn't matter, it was too small. The new place is nice and you can have a bed there."

"Can I come soon?" she says.

"Name the day."

"Wait, wait, wait, wait," my mother says. "None of this was discussed. I need to speak to you alone."

"Why alone? The message is clear and it's for everyone. I have space now, in the city, bedrooms for my kids."

"Please. May I see you, Martin?"

"Sure, I'd be glad to," my father says. "And I'd be glad to make a schedule that works for you."

"Go to sleep, Dena."

"So it's good news. Right? The kids can see the city and their father. Right, Mick?"

Her jaw stiffens as her eyes nearly close. "I told you. My name is Miriam."

Martin

THERE'S A 180-FOOT-TALL Howard Johnson's sign on the Parkway that you can see from a mile away. It stands in the parking lot of the restaurant and is surrounded by tall waving weeds and a chain-link fence. At times when my parents split, my mother took Debra and me to visit him there, a halfway point between our home and his. As I lay in bed this morning I remember how he'd light up when he saw us approach and how hard he worked at cramming as much fun into our time together as he could. But it was a diner. On the highway. So there wasn't much to do after we colored our place mats and ate lunch. The tower is where we'd go, the base of it. My father would make up stories about climbing it as a kid and ask us what we thought we could see if we climbed the ladder to the top. Debra usually said Disneyland—the castle and all the characters, a moat with black swans. Once I said, my mother, driving on the highway, coming to get us so we didn't have to stand in a parking lot all day. This hurt my father. We went a week or more without talking and I remember fearing that I'd ruined my relationship with him, just as my mother had.

I get out of bed and look out the window to see if he's left. His car is still in the driveway but it's in a different spot. Someone knocks gently on my door, then opens it. My mother is wigless and still in her nightclothes.

"I heard something downstairs," she says.

"Like what?"

"I don't know."

"Maybe it's Dad."

"Go look. Please."

It's just after six. I walk past her down the stairs and find my father fully dressed in the garage, sitting on a lawn chair near the far wall of boxes.

"Was she gonna throw these out?" he says, lifting a pile of photos from his lap. "There are pictures of me in high school in here."

"I don't know."

"This guy here, see him? This guy? Dickie Brutzman. Could throw a watermelon thirty yards from his knees."

"How long have you been out here?"

"And this is me. In the back, see?"

It's him. A teenager with dark hair but the same long straight nose. The deep-set eyes.

"Was she gonna toss these out?"

"I don't know," I say. "You should take whatever you want."

"Who throws out photographs? Your mother's a lunatic. I don't know how you live here."

This is his new line. I don't know how you live here. He's said it the last two times I've seen him.

"You should live with me," he says. "You're seventeen now, you should come live and work with me."

"Mom says I should go to college."

"Hasids don't go to college. They study Talmud and that's it."

"But I'm not a Hasid."

"College is a waste of time and money." He stands and moves around the garage, checking all the labels on the boxes. "You should come work with me."

"I think I want to be a photographer."

"Then take pictures. Walk out the front door with your camera and point the thing at life. It's everywhere. Beauty and emotion, the sky, the sea. You don't need a classroom for that."

He opens another box and flips through some records. "Dave Brubeck, Nat King Cole. Chuck Baker, Sinatra. Help me get these into the car."

In all, we put seven boxes into his trunk and backseat. He wants a standing mirror and an archery set but there isn't any room. "Maybe the mirror will fit in the passenger seat," I say.

He shakes his head. "No. Passenger seat's for you," he says.

I smile. "You know I can't go today," I say, and can already see it in his eyes. He won't let it rest.

"Go get your new camera. It's time for your first class."

"I have school."

"No, no, no. I want you to meet someone."

"Who?"

"It's a surprise."

I look down at my bare feet.

"What, you don't like surprises?"

"I drive with friends to school. I'd have to call them."

"Call them."

I look back at the house, to see if I can see my mother through the window.

"Go," he says. "Go get some clothes."

In the house, I don't see her anywhere. I throw on jeans and a T-shirt and grab my camera. I step out and onto the stairs and get halfway down before I hear her.

"Hey." My mother.

"Hey!"

"Where ya goin?"

"Dad's driving me," I yell, and keep heading toward the garage.

"David!"

I don't stop until the driveway. My dad is smoking, his back against the driver door.

"She's coming!" I say, and he flicks the butt, opens the door, and has the car started by the time I'm inside. We're in reverse and moving when she walks out the front door. Her wig is on but it's turned to the right and covering one of her ears and she's waving her arms like a maniac.

"You better stop the car," I say.

"Don't worry about it."

"She's running now, Dad."

"Don't look at her."

"Stop, *stop*!"

And he does. She comes to my window, knocks on it. I lower it.

"What's going on here?" She ducks to see my father.

"I thought I'd take the boy to work, Mick."

"First of all, he has *school*. Secondly, I told you, I do not want him in that theater."

"What makes you think I'm bringing him there?"

"You took him there the other night, Martin."

"For a few hours."

"I absolutely forbid you . . ."

"For*bid*? For*bid*, Mickey?"

"I want you out of the car, David. Now!"

"The only people who use the word 'for*bid*' are religious freaks. Is that you, honey?"

"He is seventeen years old."

"And he's spending the day with his father."

"No, he is not. He is going to school."

"Go back inside and give your daughter breakfast."

My mother reaches in the window and tries to open my door. "Do not leave this driveway. Do *not*, Martin."

"I'll have him home for dinner," he says again, putting the car in reverse. I don't look at her as we pull away, but I know she's witnessing a crime. Maybe I don't want to go. Maybe he's using me to hurt her. My father jams the accelerator when we get in the street and the tires screech as we fly down Healey Road. When I face him he puts his palm on my left knee and smiles. "See," he says, "I told you she wouldn't mind."

Brandi Lady

“Real estate” has always been the answer to “What does your father do?” Or at least the words my sister and I have used since kindergarten. On my seventeenth birthday, he took me to Shea Stadium and between innings told me the names of buildings and addresses he’d had money in since his early twenties. From Brooklyn to Queens to Manhattan and Times Square, he spoke of the friends and ex-friends with whom he’d “taken risks” since his dad had died. Shel Friedman and Gil Rottsworth and Ira Saltzman, all theater owners who ran burlesque and vaudeville shows in Times Square in the late fifties. For fifteen years they also jointly owned the Fryer Hotel, a theater on Eighth Avenue that burned down to nothing but a basement in 1970. Across the street from what remains is the Imperial, a two-hundred seater built in 1900, which my father bought with

Ira Saltzman in 1968. It was an homage to his father, Myron Arbus, who had owned a similar theater on Broadway and Forty-third from the time my dad was ten. I was there once and remember the lobby, the velvet drapery, and the enormous gold pillars that bookended the stage. A Catskill comic named Paulie Fishman pulled a quarter from his nose that day and handed it to me. The magic booger coin. There was a water cooler in the office that had cone-shaped cups and a metal dispenser. Paulie made pointy boobs with the cups and pranced around like one of the dancers. Debra laughed so hard she burped twice and Paulie mimicked her until she could hardly breathe.

I reach for my new camera to take a shot of his profile. *Click.*

"Grab some of the old pictures," my dad says.

I get a handful from the backseat and pull them onto my lap. On top is my mother, drawing whiskers on my sister's cheeks. Another sunset. More Halloween. A guy I've never seen before.

"That's my cousin Louie Bernstein," my father says, pointing. "See, he's the shmuck waving."

I show him another.

"This is . . . uh . . . her name is not coming to me. But a horrible person. *Hor*rible. Your mother's friend or cousin from somewhere, who the hell knows. She can have this one back."

The next one is my mother standing on the beach with her arms folded, gazing out at the ocean. As we pull into the Lincoln Tunnel, the traffic stops and my father takes it from my hand, staring at the picture for a while without saying a word.

"I took this," he says. "She was in her twenties. Just look at her."

"You can have it if you want," I say.

"That's not your mother anymore." He tosses it on my lap and I gaze forward into the tunnel. Like a tube-shaped pool it curves with no end in sight. As always I think of a leak, from any of the thousands of blue-tiled squares that surround us. A drip, a stream, a catastrophe. *That's not your mother anymore.* When my grandfather died, my mother was already writing three letters a week to the grand rabbi. I watched my father steal one out of the mailbox once. I told him she would find out, to put it back, but instead he opened it and read it to me. She was asking the rabbi's advice on how she should separate her children from their father, since their father refused to learn *halakhah,* Jewish law. After that, the marriage became a contest of who could outscream whom. Debra would get so upset that she'd become nauseous. I'd go into the bathroom with her and wait it out while she knelt over the toilet. Bark, bark, bark, his voice would rattle the walls, and my mother would yell back, throw things at him, tell him he'd ruined her life. It was the beginning of summer and that's when my mother packed for Maine and told me I was coming along. A two-month *baal teshuva* retreat. Me, in a black suit and yarmulke, and five hundred of my mother's new friends.

Now my father drives up Tenth Avenue and makes a right on Forty-second Street. At every light, there's either a man in a business suit, a homeless person, a prostitute or a preacher. A guy in a brown bear outfit is handing out yellow flyers. His pant legs have two big holes in the knees and one of the bear ears is missing. I try to take his picture, but we're already moving. We stop at another light and a man washes our windshield with a squeegee. My father waves his arm and flicks the wipers to stop him. Out my window is an electric bullhorn announcing a third gin and tonic free if you buy two before noon. It's seven thirty in the morning. My father parks in a lot on Forty-fourth Street. He takes a box of records and pictures from the trunk and hands me a smaller one. As I follow him down Broadway toward the Imperial, he stops short, right in the middle of the sidewalk.

"What are you doing?" I ask.

He points up at an enormous neon sign that's moored to the roof of a building on the corner.

"See this place?" he says.

"Yes."

"This is Sid Lowenstein's joint," he says. "Two *tons* of metal and glass. Just look at it, look at it. It's a cock, right?"

I didn't notice at first but, yes, it is shaped like that.

"There's only one putz in the world who would drill that many holes into the red bricks of the Marion Theatre, just to put a neon cock on it. And this, David, is why Times Square is finished. This building was one of the true beauties when I was growing up. The Marion. For years and years there was vaudeville and movies and comedians and burlesque acts in there. Now there's a fuckin' dildo shop in the lobby and a dozen peep windows, and Leo says they're making their own porn in the attic. And this is exactly what Ira wants me to do at the Imperial. He wants *this*!"

When I look up at the marquee, the thousands of bulbs ignite into a rolling upward wave of lit color that runs from the base to the tip before spurting confetti into the air above us. I watch it rain onto my palm as I try to erase the image of my father making porno movies in some attic.

"Before he went and plugged this thing in, the Marion was just like my father's old theater. All these along here, all just grand old cinemas before and into the war."

A blonde Hispanic girl walks past us and smiles as if she knows my father.

"Take it in, kid," he says, lifting his box from the ground. "Take pictures. Because one day soon, just like me, it's *all* gonna disappear."

"You busy?" the girl says to my father.

"Take a hike."

Thick white steam rises from the manholes and taxis sail through it, dragging it on their way down Broadway. Across the street is an old synagogue and next to that is what my father calls a "tit joint," the Pussycat Lounge. I smell boiling hot dogs and pretzels as a man right next to us takes a leak on a phone booth. I follow my father down the street. It starts to drizzle and then rain so I put my box on top of my head and we walk three more blocks, past pinball arcades and bars and dozens of neon twenty-five-cent peep-show signs. When I see an evangelist on an upside-down milk crate, I put the box down to take his picture. *Click.* He waves a tongue-depressor crucifix and talks directly to the sidewalk. Behind him is a bag lady with brown Magic Marker eyebrows. She smiles for the camera; her gums are tan. *Click.* When we get up to Forty-eighth and Eighth, we stand outside the Imperial and look at the marquee above the entrance. Today, the cinematic lettering reads INTERNATIONAL BURLESQUE SENSATION BRANDI LADY—MAY 3, 4 AND 5. Under that it says, HALF-PRICED WELL DRINKS—TUES. TILL CLOSING. My father and I cross the street to the front doors, where a man with a mustache is pulling on the locked door.

"Not open yet," my dad says. "Eleven o'clock."

"You're the owner," the man says. "You're Marty, right?"

My dad nods.

"I hear you're fuckin' the help, ya lucky Jew bastard."

My father puts his box on the curb. "What'd you just say?"

"Brandi Lady," he says. "Aren't you and her doin' the—"

"Hey *dick*head!" my dad says.

I put my hand on his shoulder. "Dad?"

"This is my *son*. Okay, *prick*? My son. You talk to me like that in front of my son?"

"Just let it go, Dad."

"I didn't know he was your boy, Marty."

"So you call me a Jew bastard? Who the fuck are you?"

He glances at me. "Nobody," he says. "Just a kike from Queens."

My father puts his hand on the man's chest and lightly shoves him backward. "Have some manners," he says.

Thankfully, my father unlocks the door and we're in the lobby. The first and only time I was here, the other night, there was a party in this room for my father's partner, Ira Saltzman. Now, empty, I see a much larger space than I thought, with its own chandelier that sparkles over the faded red carpet. There's a small man on his knees with a bucket near the ticket booth.

"Toilet overflowed," he says to my father. "Someone crammed a diaper in there and kept flushin'."

"A *what*?" says my father.

"Hi, I'm Jocko," he says to me. Jocko's right eye wanders and the knees of his black pants are soaked with toilet water.

"I'm David."

"Marty's boy?"

I nod.

"I heard you were here the other night."

"Just for a few minutes. My dad had to—"

"Is that him, is that David Arbus?" A huge black man with a giant bald head walks up to me. He offers his hand. "Leo. Nice to know ya. Sorry I missed you at the party. Your dad's a prince."

"I'm trying to show my kid how beautiful the theater is and I got scumbags outside and piss inside."

"We'll get it cleaned up," Leo says, looking up at the wet bubbled ceiling.

"Brandi here?" my father asks.

"Not yet," says Jocko. "Should be soon, though. Donny left for the airport a long time ago."

My father pats his pockets for his cigarettes. "Tell her I'm upstairs when she gets here. Follow me, David."

We head down a long hallway of black, ceiling-high drapery. It leads us into the stage area where a disco ball throws bits of white light onto the catwalk and walls. The aisle slopes downward like in a Broadway theater and ends at an orchestra pit and a long, empty bar. The night I was here, a dancer was on stage but no one was in the room because of the party in the lobby. I felt sorry for her as she went through her routine with no one watching. She was beautiful, of course, but I was pretty far away.

I follow my father up the stairs behind the bar to his office. As he opens the door he yells, "I knew it, I knew it! They were pullin' my chain?"

A woman wearing a tall, beehive wig the color of a fire engine is standing on his desk in a white bikini bottom. There are two matching pasties over each of her breasts and with both hands, she holds a scarlet feather.

"Brandi Lady," he says.

"Who's that?" she asks. My father steps closer to her and she hops off the table. He kisses her and holds her as he sings in a faux Yiddish accent. "Don't do that dance, I tell you, Ms. Sadie. That's not a business for a lady. Most everybody knows that I'm your loving . . ."

"Is that your son, Marty?"

"Arlene, you have no idea how happy I am to see you."

"Marty?"

"Yes, love?"

"There's a boy behind you." As he turns to me, she reaches for a bathrobe on the couch.

"My son, come meet my son."

The phone rings loudly on my father's desk and the lady lifts it in stride. "The Imperial," she says, and we both stare at her. Her eyes widen and soon she's leaning with her back arched and her hand over her forehead. She hands the phone to my father. "I'd say it's your wife."

My stomach burns as I sit on the edge of the sofa. My father puts an unlit cigarette in his mouth, then takes the phone from her hand.

"This is Marty."

Pause.

"Excuse me? What did you just call me?

Pause.

"No, what did you just call me, Mickey?"

Brandi walks over to the sofa and sits down. "Hi," she says, extending her hand.

"Hi," I say.

Her lips are wet and red and her eyelashes are longer than normal and globbed with black.

"A pornographer?" He slams the phone against his hip and returns it to his ear. "I wasn't a pornographer when you used to spend *every* dime I made, you hypocritical wanna-be *yenta*!"

He's making it worse. Name calling, screaming.

"So," Brandi says. "I hear you're a photographer."

I nod and realize I'm sitting on my camera. When I pull it out from behind me, Brandi takes it.

"Okay, give me your best pose," she says.

I turn it on for her and try to smile as my father drags the receiver away from his desk.

"Right, Mick. You got Deb and I got him."

"You look like your dad," Brandi says. "Same mouth."

"That's bullshit, I deserve to see them too."

Leo pokes his head in the door. "Was he surprised?"

"Conditions? Fuck that. What *conditions*?"

"You should have seen his eyes, Leo," Brandi says.

"Oh yeah, yeah, Mick, just like you've always said. *Your* people, *your* people. Well, ya know something? I sleep at night. Maybe it's you. Maybe you're the guilty one. Ya ever think of that?"

I can hear my mother's voice through the phone. When she gets this upset she starts to shriek.

Brandi turns and looks at my dad. "Just give her what she wants."

"Wait . . . Mickey? *Mickey*? Okay. I'm sorry. I'm sorry I said it. Are you there?"

"This time make a stupid face. Get in there, Leo, I'm takin' pictures."

Leo puts his polar bear arm around me, squeezing me into him. Brandi lifts her nostrils with her fingertips and sticks her tongue out. "Crazy like this," she says, and I stare at her tongue, long and pink like bubblegum. "Make a face," she says, and I do, my eyes crossed. *Click*.

"Fine, fine. I'll bring him. I'll bring him home this second if you agree to drop them off tomorrow."

Pause.

"Yes. Tomorrow."

Jocko comes in the room, still holding a mop and a roll of paper towels. "Was he surprised?"

"Yes!" Brandi says. "You should've seen his face."

"Yes or no, Mickey. Do you want him home or not?"

Pause.

"Then make a decision already."

Pause.

"*Two* hours? What am I gonna do in two hours? Ya gotta give me half the day. Mickey. Mickey?"

Brandi stands with the camera as my father smashes the phone down twice and glares out the window onto Broadway.

"Marty?" she says. "Can I take your picture with your boy?"

He pushes out a smirk and waits for me to walk over to him. "Of course, of course, it's just your goddamn mother had a lot to say and—"

"Forget that now," Brandi says.

"*This,* David, is who I wanted you to meet. Isn't she amazing? Just look at her."

"Put your arm around him," says Brandi.

My father pulls me toward him. "She's the real woman in my life."

"Say *cheeeeese*!"

"And the woman I'm going to marry."

I face him, but he keeps his eyes on her.

"Neither of you is smiling. David!" she says.

"Yeah?"

"Smile!"

Click.

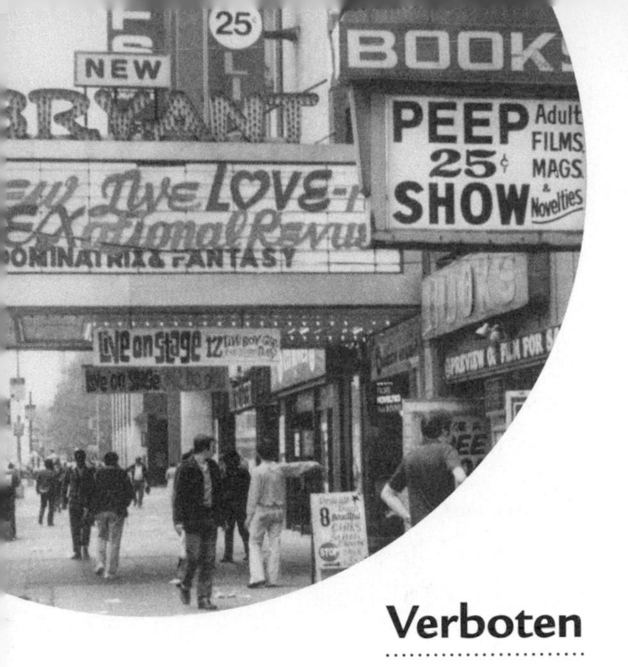

Verboten

STUDENTS OVER THE AGE *of five years and six months who are admitted to Yeshiva Bais Esther must attend* Yizkor, *a class to prepare themselves for their new lives as* baal teshuva/ *Hasids. The main text for this class is called the Shulchan Aruch, the book that lists the laws of* halakhah *that must be adhered to if one is to be worthy of Hashem's rewards (see "Rewards of* Halakhah*" in the Introduction on page xvi). The word* halakhah *comes from the Hebrew word for "going" but a literal translation equates more accurately to the phrase "the way to go." Each student must keep a log for one full year indicating his or her successes and failures as they pertain to the daily requirements of* halakhah. *"And you shall teach them the statutes and the laws, and show them the way wherein they must walk and the deeds that they must do" (Exodus 18:20).*

Students will each be given a packet to help them track their mitzvahs. *For example:*

A. I, ______, was ___successful / ___unsuccessful in adhering to the Laws of Washing the Hands in the Morning as stated in chapter 2 of the Shulchan Aruch for the week of ______, 1975.

B. I, ______, was ___successful / ___unsuccessful in in adhering to the Laws of Dressing and Conduct as stated in chapter 3 of the Shulchan Aruch for the week of ______, 1975.

C. I, ______, was ___successful / ___unsuccessful in adhering to the Laws of Proper Practices in the Lavatory as stated in chapter 4 of the Shulchan Aruch for the week of ______, 1975.

It becomes remarkably important to Leo that I receive an "initiation lap dance," before my father takes me back to New Jersey. He brings me to a small room downstairs and tells me to choose from three dancers.

"I'd rather not," I say.

"What do you mean?" Leo says.

"I don't want to."

"Sure you do."

"I was supposed to be home two hours ago."

"It just takes a minute. Tiki, Vera, or Paulette? Who do you like?"

"I'll do it next time," I say.

"Tiki wins," Leo says, guiding her over to me. Then he leaves us alone. She is the girl I saw dancing a few nights ago. Tall with brown eyes, huge breasts, and a yellow bikini with a bull's-eye on the rear. I have a boner before she sits on me and when she does I'm in trouble immediately. She's pressing her pelvic bone into my groin, actually bending my penis.

"You're Marty's boy?" Tiki says.

"Uh-huh."

Amy Posner in the ninth grade. Two minutes after we turned on the "4 O'Clock Movie," she walked out of her kitchen with no top on and yanked my pants down to my ankles. No one had ever done this to me before: *boom,* she put it in her mouth and *boom,* I finished as they say, right there, and she, I don't know, wasn't ready. Wasn't happy. It was horrific, all of it.

"Does this feel good?" she says.

"I have to go back to Jersey."

"I usually do this to music."

I shift my right leg and she slides a little and kisses my cheek. "Thank you," she says, and it's over. I'm so happy I didn't come in my pants. She stands, winks at me, and passes my father in the doorway. He leans in the room with Brandi over his shoulder.

"Let's go already," my father says. "Your mother's gonna kill me."

• • •

I GET OUT of the car in Newstead just before 9 p.m. The lie I'm considering is that I was dropped off at school and I've been at my friend Seth Greenstein's house all this time. My father honks when I get to the porch and I wave to him. A note on the door reads *At the Levitzes' for Shabbos dinner. We need to talk.*

I'm smiling when my head hits my pillow. She is not here. I am alone. No arguing, no guilt, no Jew quotes, no mother. Over and out. It's so much easier to be in this house without her. It is so much easier to be with Tiki in my mind and not in person. Her bathing suit and her skin and hair. The smell of coconut. I go into the bathroom for some hand lotion and put it on my penis. It's freezing but I try to get things going anyway. Tiki's mouth and lips and body and the coconut and how close she was to me, on me, with her tropical scent. I look at myself in the mirror, banging away, my cheeks all flushed and sweaty. It's not working. Back in my room I reach under my mattress. A *Hustler* from June 1973. The girls are so familiar now: Heather and Lily from Arizona State and all the other sorority girls of the Pac-10. Football pants on girls, yes, and Lily's having a slumber party in her dorm. Still not happening. Tiki is on me and she's grabbing my penis and I tell her to stop or there'll be trouble but she doesn't listen, nope, she just keeps on . . .

"David?"

Great. I turn my light out and roll on my side. My mother's on the stairs already. She knocks on my door but I say nothing. She opens it and the hallway light blares off my wall.

"You asleep?"

Sound asleep.

When I hear the door click closed, I shut my eyes. No arguing, no guilt, no Jew quotes, no mother. Good night.

Tiki?

Yes, David.

Let's start again.

Okay, David.

I won't shift so much.

Okay, David.

The elastic in your bathing suit is bunching. See that?

You're right. Look at that. Can you fix it, David?

I can try. I can only try.

Mickey

I WAKE UP TO MY mother sitting on a chair in the corner of my room. She allows me to blink a few times before handing me a packet of stapled papers. "Take it. Take it and read it," she says.

"I'm sleeping."

"I don't care. Read it to me. First sentence. Read it out loud."

"Mom?"

"'Students over the age,' go, read it!"

I sit up and look at it. "'Students over the age of five years and six months . . . who are admitted to Yeshiva Bais Esther must attend *Yizkor,* a class to prepare themselves for their new lives as Hasids.'"

"Keep going. 'The main text for this class . . .'"

"'. . . is called the Shulchan Aruch, the book that lists the laws of *halakhah.*'"

"Keep going."

"No."

"Please, one more line."

"I'm not, Ma. I'm sleeping."

"'These are our rules. We follow these rules . . .'"

"I know, Mom."

"I will not let you take everything I've worked so hard to build and crush it in front of my face."

"I heard you."

"You lied to me."

"I tried. I tried to get home sooner."

"You *failed*! And there's no way I'm taking you to see him today." She stands and I hear her march down the stairs.

"Was that Mom?" Debra says through the wall.

"Get dressed," I tell her.

"What?"

Downstairs I find her kneeling into the refrigerator. "Mom?"

"Not negotiable. Everything's going to change, starting today."

I have to laugh. "Today?"

She shuts the fridge and moves to the table. "Your sister wanted to know where you were all night."

"So tell her."

"Tell her? Tell her you were with your disgusting, smutty father at his *place* of business?"

"Don't blame him."

"I blame *you*," she says. "I'm just putting a stop to it."

"I forgot it was a Friday night. It got busy there and Dad had things to do."

"And I forgot it was Saturday," she says and smiles at me. "You forgot it was Friday and you came home eight hours late without calling me. And I forgot it was Saturday. I don't drive on the Shabbos, David. You and your sister won't be going to New York today."

Debra walks in, dressed, and sits at the table. "Why is everyone yelling in whispers?"

"Because Mom's made a deal with Dad," I say. "We're going into New York to see his new place today."

"Today?"

"Yup. He's excited about it. Mom made a deal last night on the phone."

My mother is glaring at me. "There is no deal."

"I was very late and I didn't call. I apologize."

"You weren't home when we left at five o'clock. You blew the deal. I don't drive on Shabbos."

I stare at the back of her football helmet–shaped wig as she walks away. An actress, that's what she is. Playing a role, wearing the costume, the pensive and protective farm girl who thinks the truth about Martin Arbus will destroy her daughter and all that she may become as an adult. The vile, revolting truth that she kept from me for thirteen years. He owns a theater. Big fucking deal. And Debra probably knows, she must know that he isn't really in "real estate." Maybe she doesn't. Maybe she's as fragile as my mother wants her to be, needs her to be, begs her to be. Your father owns a strip joint, Deb. Let's go see it. Let's go visit it together.

"So we can't go?" Debra says.

"How about the train?" I say. "We'll take the train."

"No, David," she says. "No trains either."

"Then let *me* drive."

"Just stop."

"*Mom!* Don't be a . . ."

Both of their heads pop up and glare at me.

"Don't be a *what,* David?"

"People compromise. Hasids compromise on some of the laws, they must. It's not like you're a *real Lichtiger,* right? You're an American . . . born in Nutley. Not White Russia or wherever . . . Poland. Didn't you once put gefilte fish in a bowl of matzah ball soup during a seder?"

"This is not a negotiation. You broke the trust. You betrayed me. Call your father and tell him. No one is going."

I walk to the phone and dial my father's number. There is no answer. I hang up and my mother hands me one of her leather-bound books and points to a paragraph. I know this one well. The thirty-nine categories of verboten activities on the Sabbath: *sowing, plouwing, reaping, winnowing, spinning, weaving, making two loops* . . .

"*This* is your defense? A book from the sixteenth century?"

. . . *trapping, slaughtering, flaying, writing two or more letters.*

"Not everything that is thought should be said," she says in her pious, calm tone. "And not everything that is said should be repeated."

"Just stop."

"I love you, David."

"You *love* me?"

"But you're pushing me in ways I won't be pushed."

"I *apologized* for being late."

"I want to go," Debra says. "I want to see his apartment."

"We're going," I say. "You should be able to see your father, regardless of what *I* did."

My mother walks out of the room, into the bathroom. I wait for the door to slam but it doesn't. Upstairs I grab my shoes, a sweatshirt, my mother's car keys off her dresser, and my camera. I run out to the car, start the engine, and my sister opens the front door of the house. I roll down the window to hear her.

"Me too. I want to go."

I know it's stupid but I open the door and she's in.

"I can't believe I'm doing this," she says.

I am my father. A kidnapper. I pull out of the driveway just like yesterday, just like he did.

"What am I doing?" she says.

"He wants to take you to lunch. Lunch! Okay, Deb? He loves you!"

"She loves us too," she says, looking back at the house.

"It's going to be *fun*. Forget all the other crap and let's just feel good. It's Saturday and it's nice out. Right?"

She doesn't answer me.

"Deb?"

"What?"

"I won't take you if you don't want to go."

"Just don't ask me," she says. "Just go."

"Okay. I won't ask anymore."

She nods, still staring out the window. I turn the radio on—"Crocodile Rock"—and face her. "She'll get over it."

"She'll hate me."

"No."

"I'm nervous," she says.

"Stop thinking about it. Wanna play twenty questions?"

"No."

I lower the music. "I'm thinking of an animal."

"Do you think she knows we're gone by now?"

"It's not a crime to see your father."

"We took her car."

"She's not using it. I'm thinking of an animal. Not a human. Please. Do it. Guess."

I look at the back of her head, her long dark ponytail. A sinner today, a villain, an accomplice to a crime. She tugs on her seat belt.

"Hello?" I say.

"Okay, okay," she says. "Is it a zebra?"

"No. It isn't. Ask if it lives in or zoo or something."

"Does it live in a zoo?"

"No."

"I don't care. A monkey. Do you think she knows by now?"

"No. It's not a monkey.

"Is it a cat?"

"In a way."

"Is it a tiger?"

"Yes. Wow. That's it. That was fast. It's a tiger. All right, your turn."

"I don't want to play. I have a stomachache."

"Does it live in Africa?"

"No."

"Does it have a tail?"

"No. It lives in New Jersey and its yelling my name right now, running around the house looking for me."

I laugh. "Trust me," I say, giving her shoulder a light shove. "She knows where you are."

Apartment W

"YES?" SAYS MY FATHER.

"It's David," I announce through the intercom. A long silence follows.

"You're *here*?"

"Yes. I have Debra."

"Where's your mother?"

"She let me drive."

"Into the city?"

"I did fine. I'm a good driver, Dad."

"I thought she was driving."

"Should I park?" I say.

"No, no need. I have to get out of here. I'll just get in with you."

EAST 70TH ST., the sign says and underneath in small letters, EAST JERUSALEM WAY. I somehow justify my stint as kidnapper with the Semitic-sounding street name. As if my mother would be relieved. Watching me from the car, I point out the sign for Debra but she's climbing in the back. My father emerges wearing a dark suit and a reddish tie. I don't know why he's so dressed up.

"David?" he says, from twenty feet away, and right behind him comes Brandi.

"Marty, wait, Marty!" she screams. She's running in heels, trying to get her enormous handbag over her shoulder.

"Who's that?" Debra says.

"Friend of Dad's."

My father opens the door. "Go, David," he says. "She's drivin' me nuts."

"What do you mean?"

"*Drive. Punch* it."

"You gotta wait for her, Pop."

"No, no. She's got other plans."

Too late. Brandi opens the back door and gets in next to Debra. Out of breath and wide eyed, just glaring at the back of my father's head. "Hey, asshole."

"I explained this to you, Arlene."

"Oh, *blow* it out your ear."

My father spins and points at her. "Watch your mouth. My daughter's in the car."

They look at each other and Brandi offers her hand. "I'm sorry. Hi. I'm Brandi."

"I'm Dena."

"Happy now?" my father says. "Good, be happy."

"You have your father's eyes."

"Do you mind if we go have a family day now, Arlene?"

"I'm not sitting on that couch all day, Marty."

"Then go to a movie. A museum. It's New York City, for crying out loud."

"I want to be with *you*."

"It's a goddamn *family* day. What's so hard to understand?"

"It's okay, Dad," I say. "She can come with us."

"Thank you. Thank you for saying that. Finally, a nice person."

"Where to?" I say.

Silence.

"I've heard so many wonderful things about you," Brandi says.

Debra clears her throat and sits taller in her seat. "How do you know my dad?" she says.

Here we go. Stomach burn. I glance at my father but he's looking out the window.

"We work together," Brandi says.

I see Debra nodding.

"At the Imperial."

Through the rearview my sister's eyes meet mine. I put the car in drive. No one is talking. Debra sits with her hands in her lap and my father's still sulking like a six-year-old.

"Where are we . . . uh . . . ?"

"The Queens Midtown Tunnel to the L.I.E.," he says.

"Take that to the Brooklyn-Queens Expressway and I'll guide you from there."

"Queens?" I say.

"It's a surprise, a family surprise."

"I wanted to see the apartment," Debra says.

"I'll bring you back later, baby."

"Is it your father's grave?" I ask, and he looks disappointed.

"We're going to a cemetery?" says Brandi.

My father turns to her. "What? You don't like the plan now?"

"You never said a cemetery, Marty."

"You can *wait* in the car, Arlene. The Queens Midtown Tunnel."

"Where's that?" I say.

"Just go straight. Turn right at the corner."

"I really hate cemeteries," Brandi says, and my father starts shaking his head.

"I do too," my sister says.

"It's Saturday, Marty. And we've got the kids. Let's go the beach, Jones Beach."

For a moment all I hear is the sound of the highway. I try to think of a question to ask, to dilute the tension.

"Maybe Debra and I will go shopping instead," says Brandi.

"Terrific," my father says. "Just leave her with me and you go right ahead."

I find Debra in the mirror, smiling. Brandi sits forward

on the seat and faces her. "Can I see what your hair looks like when it's down?" she says.

Debra shrugs and looks at my father.

Brandi reaches to remove the ponytail holder. "Just for a second. It's so beautiful."

The hair comes down over her shoulders. My father turns to see it and can't help but grin. "My God," he says, "You *are* your mother."

Brandi fluffs it like a hairdresser and reaches for her purse. "I know we've just met," she says.

It's lipstick that comes out first. I wait for Debra to reject the idea, but she doesn't. What I see in the rearview is a fifteen-year-old Hasidic girl with her lips puckered and ready. Eight seconds in the car with Brandi Lady and the Jew laws get tossed out the window.

"Does it come off easily?" Debra asks.

"Oh yes," Brandi says, uncoiling the stick. "It's the eyeliner we'll have to scrub at. Okay . . . face me . . . lips like this . . . good . . . perfect. Don't move. And here we go."

It's a Boy

THE CEMETERY IS CALLED LIEBERMAN and Wise. It's set on a very green and mildly sloped hill that blocks the sight of a gun range on one side. A new addition to the neighborhood apparently. The popping of rifle bullets is sporadic and relatively banal but a strange sound to hear in a field of headstones. My father leads us up a narrow path of small white rocks and leans over to touch a plaque on the grass. "Joseph Tuschsky was my dad's partner," he says. "The theater they bought was called the Drake, July 1929. I was ten."

Brandi steps toward my father, puts her hand on his shoulder. "Happy birthday, Mr. Arbus."

"This is *Tusch*sky," my father says. "I'm telling a story about Joe Tuschsky. Can't you read?"

"Yes . . . I can read, Marty. Jesus, you're right back at it, aren't ya?"

"Arlene, please."

"Where's your father's plot?"

"He's over there, we'll go in a second, I'm telling a story."

"Then go ahead."

They are a strange couple. The Borscht-belt Jew and his Marilyn Monroe. When I look at my sister she's twenty-two years old with the lips and the eyes and her hair now brushed. I take my camera out, and point it at her. *Click.*

"Don't, David, don't," she says, holding her palm out the exact way my mother always does.

"You look good."

"Liar."

"You look *normal.* Give me a pose."

"Please don't take my picture."

I move toward her with the camera high and she squeals and runs behind my father. *Click, click, click,* her face lit up with joy.

"I'm telling a story."

"Tell him to stop."

"Can you let her be, David?"

"Sorry."

"Tuschsky was connected in Los Angeles. He had an uncle who produced movies, cowboy-type movies, and when he died the contact stayed fresh because of another man named Don Micklin."

"Is he here too?" Brandi asks.

"No! He lives in West Palm Beach."

My father raises and drops his arms, then walks about

fifty yards up the path we're on. "That's him, right there, you can see the name. You don't want to hear the whole story, I don't care."

We all get close to the plot and Brandi kneels to touch the engraving. "Happy birthday, Mr. Arbus," she says. "I hear you were quite a man."

A deep, deep breath from my father. "You both have about ten relatives on this plot, not including my mother. She wanted to be in Jersey with her sisters. My aunt Gertrude, my father's sister, is somewhere out there, toward those sycamores, along that fence there, ya see where I mean?"

"What's that sound?" Debra says. "Fireworks?"

I point the camera at my grandfather's plot. The engraving, the yellowed grass, the small stones left on top. *Click.*

"Micklin and my father got first-run movies for years. Tell me if I've told you this story already. I ran the projector with Chaplin and Errol Flynn films and everything Lionel Barrymore did in those days."

"Lionel Barrymore?" Brandi asks.

"The contact wouldn't run dry until the early forties and my father and Uncle Joe started getting films from another source. I'd be the one who went and picked the canisters up at a trucking yard in Jersey City."

A family of five walks by us. The man and the boy wear yarmulkes. "*Shabbat shalom*," the man says to my father, who ignores him.

"*Shabbat shalom*," Debra responds.

"Tuschsky was very kind to me, never once treated me like a kid. He was a big drinker and he liked to gamble all day but that son-of-a-bitch was never afraid to put his arm around me and even used to kiss me . . . on my forehead. Something my father would never ever do."

My dad kneels on the grass before his father's plot. "Happy ninety-first birthday, Papa."

Brandi steps closer to him and waves Debra and me toward her. It's awkward for me. Staged sentimentality. I don't really move but then my sister's hand is out and I take it and we all end up behind my dad.

"Family is the only thing that matters. These two people right here are my children. Your beautiful grandchildren," he tells the stone. "You met David a while back but he's changed a lot. He's a man now. Look at him. I know he's gonna make me so proud out there . . . with his old man. And *this,* this person over here is my girl. I don't get to see her as much as I used to, as much I need to. My God, she's growing up so fast, Papa."

Debra bends to hug him, and I wish I'd done that too.

My father is silent for a minute and stands, his cheeks lined with tears. "Okay," he says, "I love ya, and I just wanted to say hello and happy birthday. So, good-bye for now. We're gonna go do something fun. Right?"

"Right!" says Brandi.

We walk back down the path toward the car and I notice that Debra and Brandi aren't next to us. When I look back at them their faces are so close, their noses practically touching. I lift my camera and decide to call this one *The Hasid and the Stripper. Click*. Top five this week:

5. *Smashed TV*
4. *Styrofoam Wig Head*
3. *Old Man with Hand in Garbage Can*
2. *Burnt Orange Sun Setting between Skyscrapers*
1. *The Hasid and the Stripper*

"David," my father says.

"Looks like Deb and Brandi are friends," I say.

"Yeah, yeah," he says. "She can be a nightmare, that one. You wouldn't believe what she was laying on me all night."

"What do you mean?"

"Go ask her. It's what we were fighting about. Or go ask Ira. He'll tell you."

"Why can't you tell me?"

"They want to upgrade, like everyone else, just go and turn the place into a goddamn peep show. Big plans, big ideas, put the film peeps in, the live peeps in, just turn it all into a big fuckin' gyno exam. I tell them over and over, nothing brings the scum in faster than the peeps, but they don't care, they see dollar signs in their sleep. And Abromowitz, this shmuck I've known forever, has Ira wanting to buy his inventory. Guy's in the dildo biz. I told him I'd come over tomorrow but I'll tell you right now, I'm not a opening my wallet for shit. You should come with me. It'll be good for ya."

"Dad?"

"What?"

"I have no idea what you're talking about."

"We're in the mood to see some boys," Brandi says. "Debra says she wants to get whistled at."

"No, I don't," she says. "I never said that."

"Arlene, don't turn my little girl into someone she's not, okay?"

"Little girl? She's not exactly a baby."

"Let's get back to city," my father says. "How 'bout a movie?"

Debra's smile fades as she glances at me. "I think we'd better get back to Newstead."

"What?"

"The car, mom's car," I say. "She wouldn't drive us, ya know, the Sabbath and all. I ended up taking it without, really . . ."

"What are you telling me?" He looks at Brandi, his eyes blinking. "What did he just say?"

"I think he said he took the car."

"It's Shabbat," Debra says. "We don't drive."

"We borrowed it," I say. "I'll call her. I'll call her right now."

My dad has his hands on his head. "From *where*? She can't pick up the phone anyway. *Christ,* David. That was stupid. Get in the car. *I'm* driving, move over. Move!"

"It'll all work out," Brandi says.

"You know who's gonna pay for this. *Right?*"

I look at my father as I get in the passenger seat. "Sorry."

"Yeah, me too!"

Debra looks chastened and stressed. She starts rubbing off the lipstick with the back of her hand. It's smears up onto her cheeks and nose and now her sleeve.

"Um . . . that's not really how I'd do that," Brandi says, looking for a tissue in her purse. "Stay still. Let's keep it off your clothes."

"And off your mother's car," my father says, sitting up to find her in the rearview. "She looks like she's been punched, Arlene."

"Stay still," says Brandi. "Let me get your eyelids."

"She'll probably call the cops."

Grand theft auto. Kidnapping. Speeding. Cursing. Hating. I'll tell them I was inspired by my own father. He also ignored her and we flew out of there, leaving the smell of rubber on the driveway. I ignore her and I'm going to jail. Why'd you do it, kid? Why'd you steal your mama's car? Because she's a killer of fun. A murderer of energy and glee. She says *no*, you *can't*, the same way her grand rabbi says she can't and won't and shouldn't and, "*Don't!*"

I just yelled that as loud as I could.

My father's eyes are pinned on me. "Don't what?"

It's impossible to miss her. She's the first thing we see when my father pulls up to the curb on East Jerusalem Place. Standing outside the passenger door of a running taxi, her face a furious stone.

"Be calm," Brandi says. "You've done nothing wrong."

"You don't understand," Debra says.

"Help her with her hair," I say. "Where's the tie?"

"Don't tell me you lost it, Arlene."

"I didn't lose it," Brandi says. "Oh, here it is, here it is."

When my mother sees us she points at the windshield and quickly walks our way.

My father's out of the car first, his hands in the air. "Hey there, gorgeous. I heard there was a misunderstanding."

"Give me the keys, Martin," she says, and stabs me with her eyes as I exit the car.

He hands them to her and she walks to the driver's seat and gets in. "Get out," she says to Brandi.

"You must be Mickey."

"Will you please get out of my car?" my mother says.

Brandi steps out and walks over to my dad and me. My mother starts the car.

"Mickey," my father yells. "This is ridiculous. Let me say good-bye to my daughter."

She goes into a hard U-turn that she can't make and then tries a K-turn, fighting with the steering wheel and jolting forward like a bumper car. She finally straightens out and drives by us.

"Mickey! You're forgetting your son!"

"*Keep* him!" she yells, and I run after the car.

"Finally!" I scream at her. "Thank God! Free of all the *bullshit*."

As the car pulls away, I stand there in the street, watching it go. My father's got an unlit cigarette between his teeth and he's bouncing on the tips of his toes and smiling.

"I guess I'll stay here tonight," I say.

"Don't think I've ever seen her this mad."

"She was shaking," Brandi says. "Her cheeks were shaking."

My father lights the cigarette and laughs on the exhale. "See, Arlene. You don't need a baby after all. Congratulations!" he says, and points at me. "It's a *boy*!"

THERE ARE NO extra sheets yet or a blanket or pillow, but Brandi helps me figure it out. She finds an afghan and some towels in a box in the closet and gives me a pillow off my dad's bed. The apartment is empty of a sofa or a television or any type of table, really, and doesn't appear to have any signs of habitation, other than a toaster oven and a few empty ice trays in the freezer. There is, on a bookshelf in my room, my father's Who's Who collection of books, which has always been important to him, even though I've never see him read them. *Who's Who in America, Africa, Germany, France, Spain, Canada,* and so on, probably thirty books.

As I lay on my makeshift bed I think of my sister. How bad was it? The questions. The consequences. The discipline according to God. Maybe nothing happened. Not a word, not a glare, not a mention of me. Just a broom to sweep it somewhere safe and out of reach, like so much in her life. I miss my room. And the things I wish I had here. Is this for real? I tell myself my mother still loves me and decide it doesn't matter. Maybe I don't love her. But that isn't true. I take a picture of the ceiling and my shoes in the corner. I take a picture of my pants on the radiator in this otherwise empty bedroom. I take a picture of *Who's Who in Arabia*. I don't have any clothes here or even a toothbrush. There are two Instamatics in my closet at home and my tripod and camera bag and all my cassettes and albums. There's my *Hustler* under my bed and a tiny bag of weed in my bottom desk drawer I got from Seth Greenstein, who's going to wonder where I am on Monday morning. My mother will have all of it in a box in the garage by tonight. I get up and call her, to make sure she stays out of my room. No one picks up. I don't even have a shirt to wear tomorrow. Why the hell does she get to decide where I live? It rings and rings and finally I hang up. But then I call again and again and again. No one ever picks up. I go back to my bed and lay there and can't sleep. I open *Who's Who in Germany*: SCHAPER, Wolfgang, physiologist, born in Oschersleben, Jan. 11, 1934. SCHARF, Albert, broadcasting, born in Munich, Dec. 28, 1934. I hear music from the apartment below me, and mumbled voices, the drone of a TV. I look at the white walls and the sliding mirror on the closet door and tell myself I want to be here. What does she mean, "Keep him"? Keep him, she says, like she's giving away a gerbil. I get up and call yet again. Fifteen rings, sixteen rings. She must know it's me.

Strap-a-Long

My father knocks on my door at 7 a.m. and for a minute I have no idea where I am.

"Get showered and dressed, we're goin' to Larry's."

I don't find out who Larry is until we're in the car. He's a childhood friend of my father's who owns a "toy store" on Forty-sixth Street. My father speaks a thousand miles per hour, and has an I ♥ New York coffee mug in his hand as he drives.

"Ira never calls this much and never wants to meet, but two weeks ago one of his connected friends wants to show him what the competition is doing so he takes him into Spanky's and Killowatt and Show World and it changes everything. Ira ends up wanting more than a straight burlesque theater because he's positive we're going to be swallowed whole by the peeps but I remind him that the

Imperial has always kept its 'integrity.' That's the word I use, one little word that sets him off like a Nazi at a bar mitzvah. I mean he goes fuckin' ballistic on me and starts yelling and having a coronary about what the investors are saying about me and how we're losing money and what the strip is today and fuckin' Betamax sales and I tell him to calm the hell down and he says, 'Upgrade this fucker *yesterday*, Martin!' So I tell him to get out. To go get some fresh air or some scotch and stop talking to me like one of his fat stupid stepchildren. I watch him huff down the street from my office window and think about my father and what he'd say if he were here listening to old Ira spitting and yelling and what he'd do to me if he saw a bunch of dildos hanging in the Imperial Theatre like a row of dead geese in some chink restaurant. A day later Ira has Larry Abromowitz call me, a guy I've known since Hebrew school in Hell's Kitchen. 'I'm dumpin' the strap,' he tells me. 'I want you to have it. The missus has colon cancer and we're moving to a condo in Boca.' So I feel bad now, I've known his wife for years, went to their wedding, and I tell him I'm very sorry about it all and wish you all the luck in the world, but I don't want to be in the toy biz. He says to me, Ira said you wanted it. I say Ira's full of shit. Larry says you're outta your mind, the stuff's been flying off the shelves for a full year now. Bullshit. And I mean bullshit. The guy's always been full of shit. I remember when he was nine years old and he stuck a pencil eraser in his ear and popped his eardrum. I mean I knew he wasn't headed to NASA the day I met him.

Big surprise, he becomes a salesman in Times Square right out of high school. Sells all that *tchotchke* crap for years, mounds of fake shit and magic tricks and posters of Houdini and stuff like that. Then it was pinball machines and theater tickets and every goddamn drug you can think of. In the sixties he sold grass by the pounds out of the second floor attic and downstairs was a tourist trap that had King Kong T-shirts and postcards and shit like that. So now it's dildos. And strap-ons. And who knows what else. Good for you, Larry, you little-dicked Heeb. Your mother must be so proud."

We park in the same lot as we did the other day and find Leo waiting for us outside a diner called Tilt and Hammer on Forty-third Street. Six feet whatever and just monstrous around the shoulders and neck, Leo has a tiny piece of pink tissue blotting a shaving nick near his chin.

"Where we goin' so early?" he says, his hands buried in the pockets of his khakis.

"Strap-a-Long," my father says to him. "A toy store."

Leo nods and grins. "We buyin' her?"

"I hope not."

We all head up the six blocks on Broadway and Leo points to the sign: STRAP-A-LONG-CASSIDY in cursive black neon.

"Is that you, Martin?" a man yells as he walks out to greet us. "*The* Martin Arbus?"

"Hello there, Larry. You're lookin' a little older."

"Aren't we all, aren't we all."

The top three buttons of his wide-collared shirt are open so his five-pound gold *chai* can glow in the field of white chest hair. He embraces my father like it's Passover and Leo and I shake his hand. "This way, boys, the tour starts here."

Inside the store I see rows and rows of brightly lit shelves and walls of porn magazines. There's a smell I can't pinpoint but it's a little like ammonia and wet dog. Gross. A man wearing bike shorts and an American flag tank top smiles at me before heading into a back room.

"Wait up," I say, catching up to Leo.

He's lifts a floppy pile of black leather straps off a discount table and turns to Abromowitz. "What does this do?" he says.

Larry helps him get the thing over his head but pulls shy of placing the ball gag in his mouth. Leo laughs, nods, blushes as he tries to get it off. There are hundreds of items here. A candy store for horny adults. My first thought is there's no way to picture this mush of color and pink plastic inside the lobby of my dad's theater. The signs above us are in red glitter. FOR HIM—FROM HER. FOR HER—FROM HIM. FOR HER—FROM HER. FROM HIM—FOR HIM. ONE PRONG. TWO PRONGS. THREE PRONGS?

Larry's right arm is out and swirling like one of those girls on a game show and he's lost in a spiel about women coming in from Jersey and eventually my dad's had enough.

"Time out!" he screams, with his hands a T.

"What's the matter?"

"I don't want to be rude . . . but . . . this isn't gonna work for me."

"What's wrong?"

"Larry, I wouldn't even be here if it weren't for Ira. So I'll send *him* over and you can give *him* the tour. Okay? I'm not trying to be rude but . . . can you imagine my father's face, Larry, if he thought I was buying you out."

Larry steps closer to my father. "It's like I said, Marty, I made a *mint* this year. Housewives alone. A fuckin' mint. It's a new phenomenon. They wrote about it in the *Times*. They come from all over. Even Philly."

"Then keep it."

"We're off to Boca, Marty. By the end of the month."

"Right."

"Don't make up your mind so fast. Look around. I got movies too. Please, just look."

Leo and I follow Larry deeper into the store but my father stays behind with his hand on his forehead. Leo and I can't help giggling, bumping each other like kids, touching the rubber tit on a human doll. INFLATABLE MEN, WOMEN AND PECKER. NO HOLE LOVE DOLLS FOR YOUR MOUNTING PLEASURE!

"Welcome to your bondage and sadomasochistic wing," Larry says. "To the left, a smorgasboard of nipple clamps and whips and canes for the spanking. And over this way you got your blindfolds, collars, cuffs, and masks."

When I face Leo he's reading the back packaging on a torpedo-sized dildo.

"Female- and animal-shaped love dolls, discreet masturbator pocket pals and blow-up pornstars. Either a you boys want to touch Seka's ass?" Larry laughs with his head back and I can see every filling he's ever received.

"And I got movies too. Real cheap, big stars. You runnin' film peeps yet, Martin? Where's Martin?"

"No," says Leo. "We're not showing peeps."

"Jesus, man. What's the holdup? How you guys making any money over there? I got over a thousand feet of stag films you could loop in an afternoon. I'm talkin' good fresh stuff. Girl-boy, girl-girl, I got teens."

"I gotta run," my father says, as he comes in the room. "You're gonna sell this in a heartbeat, Lawrence. You're right, it's very special. I'm happy for ya. Tell Ruth that I hope she feels better soon. I wish I was goin' with ya. Where in Boca exactly?"

"You didn't see the magazines yet?"

"Don't need to, Larry."

"Just let him show us," Leo says.

"Come back with Ira. I'm done here."

We follow my father back toward the exit down a different aisle. ANAL BEADS, BALLS, BULLETS AND EGGS.

Larry jogs up to my dad and puts his arm around his shoulder. "Martin, I'm in a little bit of a jam. I got to sell the store. Ruth is very, very sick."

"I know. I know, Larry. You told me. But the thing is this, ya see—"

"I'll give it to you for *half* the asking. Half, Martin. A *steal*. But only if you take it off me this week."

My father steps out of the store and onto the sidewalk. I can't tell if he's considering the offer or trying to get away. He starts down Broadway and without looking back lifts his hand, waves and yells, "I'll call you!" We follow him.

It's not the friendliest area in the world so I'm sort of pleased to be with Leo. We keep passing quivering bodies in doorways and people with bruised, outstretched hands. At one point Leo is approached by a man in a skirt with tennis-ball boobs who's lifting his white miniskirt to show us his panties. He flickers his fat, brown tongue at us. Leo bumps the guy, who stumbles hard, nearly tasting the curb.

"Fuckin' bitch!" the tranny screams, then reaches into a trash can, winds up his arm, and throws a bottle in a brown paper bag. He hurls it like I throw lefty and it breaks without drama on the sidewalk. Leo runs at him and the guy takes off into the street.

When we catch up to my dad, he's talking as if we've been with him the whole time.

"'Keep up with the Joneses,' Ira says. 'When in Rome,' Brandi says. All they really want to do is kill everything beautiful and sensual and bring scumbags in to jack off in my theater with their pants at their ankles. Fuck that!"

"Then don't buy it," I say. "Keep it the way you want it. Don't have a heart attack over this. Right, Leo?"

Leo doesn't answer. My father waits and waits and then faces him. "Leo?" he finally says.

"We need 'em," he says. "Film peeps and live peeps. If we want to stay open near the strip."

"Bullshit," my father says.

"Who's gonna come, boss? There are better spots around the corner. You said it yourself, people buying up leases on the strip for what? Five grand or more for six hundred square feet? If we don't pull our weight in the spot then—"

"Funny, Leo. I thought you were one of the holdouts. You been talking to Ira? Or Brandi?"

"The thing is, boss, we're losing money. Forget Ira for a second. Tokens and the peeps are where it's at. Burlesque? Burlesque is dead."

"Oh it is? It is, Leo? I can name three spots in Atlantic City that run purely on burlesque."

"But this is here. We're talking about here."

My father says nothing for the rest of the walk back to the Imperial. When we get inside, there's a silver-haired man with an orange tan standing in the lobby with Brandi and two other men. It's Ira. Ira Saltzman. I saw him the other night but he didn't see me. He has lips the color of veal for some reason and they're puffy, like he's been sucking on a lozenge. He shakes my father's hand but not Leo's.

"You're interrupting a good story. Where was I?"

One of the men reminds him. "You said the state . . ."

"That's right, it's the state who says that by *law* a theater presenting a drama or a comedy has to charge sales tax on each ticket. The loophole for us: musical performances are exempt. At stake is a quarter million dollars in back taxes. I can't believe my ears so I say what's the problem and this fuckin' tax prick over there says you're not a musical, you're a *porn* theater. I look right in his eyes and ask him how I'm supposed to operate without music. Can you tell me that, shmuck? He says, 'That's not my problem, sir.'"

Ira smacks himself on the forehead. "'Not your problem?' I say. 'Fuck you!' I'm tellin' ya, I was gonna murder this cue stick, right there, with my fuckin' hands."

All of them laugh and laugh and as it dies down, the other men greet my father with handshakes.

Ira puts his hand on my dad's back. "We didn't know what happened to you, Marty. Saul thought you fell through a manhole."

"I'm here, I'm here. I didn't realize all the troops were coming today. This is my boy, David."

I meet Roger Goldman, Harvey Casher, and Corky Lehman. Ira has his fingertips on Brandi's lower back and I can see that it's making my father nuts. She's in a very tight evening gown of blood red sequins and there's a matching top hat that rests tilted on top of her wig. She isn't speaking or even acknowledging me so I say, "Hello," and she smiles, as if not wanting to crack the makeup on her cheeks.

"Hi," she says. "I can hardly breathe in this dress."

We all walk into the empty theater and Leo, heading to the bar, asks what everyone is drinking. We sit at one of the

VIP circular tables that's placed in the open nook of the C-shaped stage, about two feet from the edge of the pit. Ira laughs and puts the tip of his thumb on Brandi's chin. He turns her head toward me.

"See that kid over there with the hair. I knew him when he wasn't yet a foot tall and still crapping himself. He doesn't remember me but I came to his bris."

"I remember you," I say.

"From the *bris*?" All the men laugh.

"No. After that. You gave me a giant stuffed monkey. A Curious George."

My father loosens up and grins at me. "So that's where that guy came from."

"Of course, me, I bought it. Your uncle Ira bought it. You done with high school?"

I nod. "Three weeks."

"Where you headed to college?"

I look at my dad. "Don't know."

"Don't know? Don't know? Marty, you skimpin' on the most important time in the boy's life?"

"College is for suckers," my father says, and I wonder how many times I've heard him say it. "One of the biggest scams of our time."

"ANYBODY OUT THERE?" says a voice from the sound booth above, a man my father calls Soundman Sal. "Welcome to the world famous Imperial Theatre. You're in for quite a private treat this morning because our first dancer's come all the way from San Francisco to get you hot, hot, hot. So let's hear a nice round of applause for the sexy and sultry Tiki Nightly."

Her music is "Susie Q" by Creedence and it's cranked to an almost eardrum-piercing level. My father isn't happy. He stands, signaling with his thumb for Sal to turn it down. On stage now is Tiki in a blue nightgown-like thing and a wig that reaches to her butt. She winks at me and is already on her knees and crawling toward us. With my father still motioning, the music lowers but only slightly. Ira pulls his chair closer to mine. "So you remember the monkey I got ya, right?"

I nod. "It's in my garage."

My father lights a cigarette. "Just found a ton of pictures in the garage," my father tells him. "The Acapulco trip. Remember that? With the parrots, in that place?"

Ira nods and smiles. "What was it, '56, '57?"

"I was gonna say it was 1960 because Mickey was there."

"Mick the quick," Ira says, and my father glances at me, embarrassed.

Tiki leans over the end of the stage and points at Harvey. He laughs, reaching for his wallet. Four singles land at her feet and she pulls the nightgown over her head and hurls it. It lands on Harvey's shoulder.

"Where are the pictures?" Ira yells as Tiki swings over us, gripping the gold pole.

"She's wonderful!" says Harvey. He searches for more cash and this time finds a five. Tiki sits on the end of the stage, legs spread. Suddenly Brandi isn't interested anymore. She dramatically turns her back to Tiki and her very open legs, wanting all of us to know she's not impressed. The stripteaser versus the stripper. Brandi looks at my dad, who's leaning to his right, trying to hear Ira.

"This girl's a stupid whore," Brandi says, reaching for her cigarettes. "Nine bucks on the stage and she's showing off her cervix."

Leo arrives with drinks and brings me a beer.

"David," my father says. "Run upstairs to my office and grab the pictures of Ira in Acapulco. They've gotta be in one of the boxes."

"I'll go," Brandi says.

"No, no, it's okay," I say, as Tiki goes down on all fours for Harvey, aiming her ass cheeks at the rafters. I head for the stairs, where the music is lower, and pass two other girls watching Tiki do her thing. In my father's office, on the wall to the right of the door, are about fifty or more signed photographs of various burlesquers and some men too, like Lou Goldstein, the Simon Says King of Grossinger's. Some are black and white and nearly all are posed shots, the women in frilly feathered garb, their heads back, shoulders exposed.

The boxes are in the closet, just where we left them. To find Ira in here might be impossible. I lift a pile and thumb through them: Debra with pail on beach, Debra in yellow bathing suit with kitten on the front. My mother asleep, someone at a pumpkin patch, my dad in high school, a woman I don't know, more Deb on the beach. A woman in silhouette, another woman kneeling, lifting money from a stage—she's in a headdress and the pieces, the feathers are lit at the tips with a distant blue light. The woman has my mother's face, the profile too, and it's in these seconds that it all becomes clear to me. The veins behind my knees start tingling as I lift the picture up to my face.

It's her. It is. She's got a thick, shiny layer of makeup on, cartoonish eyelashes. Her breasts look huge and her legs are way longer than they are. "It's her," I say, to no one in the room. "It's you." Of course. My first thought is to confront her. To find her and hand the Polaroid to her. I stuff the picture in the front of my pants and turn out of the office. The very moment I put my foot on the staircase, my ankle turns and I'm falling and rolling and trying to stop myself but can't. Whew, when I finally settle, I have my back up against the wall and I'm not quite at the bottom. My mother was a stripper. Jesus Christ. The two girls from before are there and helping me stand.

"You okay?" one says as I make my way down to my father. Tiki is sitting on Harvey's lap. On stage is a black woman in a Cleopatra outfit and the music is "Boogie Shoes." Ira is whispering into Brandi's ear and my father has his drink tipped to his mouth.

"I couldn't find it," I say, close to his ear.

"Not one of Ira?" he asks.

"I need to borrow your car."

"What?"

"I need to go get my things from home, some clothes and my cameras. I don't have anything."

He nods and puts his hand on my cheek. "I'll get you some clothes. You should probably stay away from Jersey for a while. Aside from school. I'll take you to school in the morning."

"I don't need new clothes. I have clothes at home. Let me go get them."

Cleopatra is walking down the steps of the stage, pointing at me. When I look up, Ira and Harry are laughing because I'm backpedaling away from her, away from being part of the shtick. She reaches me anyway and wraps a yellow, glittery rope around my torso. My shoulder aches from my fall.

"Hello, slave," Cleopatra says into my ear, and I say, "I can't now," and she says, "Are you a bad slave?" and I say, "No," and she puts her lips on my ear. Boner. She kisses me on the cheek and sort of taps me on the zipper of my pants. I jump back and hear Brandi yell, "Get back on stage!" My father reaches in his pocket and pulls out his car keys. "Be quick," he says, throwing them to me. "Lickity split."

I CAN SEE the two of them in my mind, meeting at the theater for the first time. She was eighteen years old when she auditioned and he liked her body, her face, her long and wavy brown hair. She didn't talk to the other girls and it made them not like her. But the boss liked her and that made the others even more resentful. The boss would drive her home, buy her coffee before he dropped her off. One night he kissed her and they ended up going to his apartment. They made me that night but she didn't know it was me until she was dancing a few weeks later, kneeling to lift the cash that had been tossed on the stage. She felt nauseous when she dipped her knees, felt sick and stupid because she knew what it meant, this feeling inside her, and she hated herself for letting this happen. Me, growing inside of her, waiting to come out and flip her life into something unwanted. My father took her picture as she knelt. She didn't look at him. What now? A house in the 'burbs of Jersey, a wedding ring, promises of familial bliss and barbeques and neighbors with bowls of sugar. And when I was born, my father held me and kissed me and said, wow, he's got my eyes before handing me back to my mother and leaving the house until 4 a.m. every night. The other moms at the playground said you need another, you have to have another, a girl would be perfect so this one can learn to share. So she asked the boss and he rolled his eyes and reminded her that the baby keeps you up all night. She said no, it's you, you, the man who brought me here, the man who never comes home that keeps me up at night and they fought and called each other names and he said I'm not coming back and she said please, don't say that, I'm lonely here in this big house and he said I'm sorry, but I have to work and she cried and cried and wished there was someone else to call, to talk to, a mother of her own. But she hates her mother, has never to this day mentioned her name or anything about her except the fact that she died alone in a nursing home which my uncle Don paid for. My father said, "I know, I got it." She said she was lonely, right? He brought the party home. She dreaded the people. Always. But she went through the motions—the drinks, the fake laughs, the charade of friendship, all of it. Until she couldn't anymore. She told him she wanted a divorce. He agreed and said he'd go. She became depressed. She called him frantically. So he moved back in. And then they had a girl.

As I drive, I look at the picture again. She looks cold. She's got nothing on her legs.

I park in the street and stare at my house. I'll hand her the photo before I say hello. Or I'll say hello, how are you, I found something I thought you'd like to have. I could laugh as I give it her, as if, hey, no big deal. *Is that how you and Dad met? That's crazy. You never mentioned you were a bottomless stripper, not ever, how weird. You said you met Dad at a party, remember, a party.* There's no car in the driveway. The house looks empty. My keys are inside the house so I try a few that are on my father's keychain but none works. The window over the sink is locked. I try the garage door and it's open. There's the giant stuffed monkey that Ira bought me, sticking upside down in one of the soggier boxes. I pull it out by the foot, take it with me into the house, and up to Debra's room. I prop George up on her bed and bend one of his knees before tying his arms in a knot. The Polaroid I place on his lap.

My sister will walk in and freeze when she sees it. "Who's that?" she'll call out to my mother. It's George, my mother will say. No, I mean in the picture. Who's that woman in the picture? That's me, when I was younger, stripping, naked, in front of men.

You were a stripper? Yes. What if Becca finds out? Or Rachel or Miriam or Gilda or Chaya or any of the other ladies find out that you were a boom-boom girl? Won't that hurt us? Won't they tell the others? You've got to hide this. You've got to hide this forever.

All my clothes and cassettes and albums and two cameras and the *Hustler* and a tripod and Seth's dime bag fit into my green army bag. The duffel ends up being too heavy to carry so I drag it out into the hallway, down the staircase, out the front door and across the lawn to the street.

"David?" It's our neighbor Mrs. Litvak sweeping her driveway. When I was thirteen she saw me peeing on the Healey's rhododendrons because Bruce Hallard dared me to do it. Mrs. Litvak told my mother and my mother made me walk over and apologize to Rona Healey. Rona Healey made me hose down her rhodies.

"You must be graduating soon," she yells.

I nod.

"Congratulations. Where are you headed in the fall?"

"I don't know," I say, shrugging. "Maybe photography school."

"My nephew just got into Yale," she says, and waits for a reaction.

I have nothing to say. I'm thinking of the Polaroid on George's lap, of my sister seeing it, walking toward it, lifting it to her face.

"Are you looking for your mother?" she says.

"Yes. Do you know where she is?"

She comes to the sidewalk, dragging the broom behind her. "They're in Vincent today. She said it was some kind of brunch."

The Danowitzes.

"Thanks," I say, closing my dad's car trunk. I look up at the windows of my sister's room and start to feel wrong about leaving it up there. I head to the driveway, return to the house, and grab the picture. When I get to the car, Mrs. Litvak hasn't moved an inch.

"Where did you say you were headed in the fall?" she asks.

"Uh, Harvard," I say. "Harvard University."

Her palm is placed over her mouth before she applauds right there. I watch the broom fall onto her fluffy grass. "*Mazel tov*," she says. "Your mother must be going crazy!"

I smile at her as I get back in the car. "You have no idea."

Kallah

MY FATHER CALLS THE TOWN of Vincent, New Jersey, "Heebville." It has all the sects: the Satmars, the Lichtigers, the Sephardics, the Ashkanzis, and who knows how many more there are. The Danowitz house is like all the others on their block—an A-frame with beige aluminum siding and a yellowish front lawn the size of a picnic blanket. I've been to the Danowitzes three or four times but not since Mr. Danowitz, known to his daughter as Peter Rabbi, told me I was "killing my mother" by not embracing *halakhah*. Sarah, who is Peter Rabbi's daughter and Debra's closest Hasidic friend, told me that her father denies every aspect of his life before becoming a *baal teshuva*. Fifteen years ago he was "without God," teaching world history at Fordham University, never having even gotten bar mitzvahed, which he did, finally, in his midthirties. It's as if he's humiliated by his own past, his own memory and that's why Sarah calls him Peter Rabbi, to remind herself that he was once just a Peter before he became a Pinchus. My mother was a Mickey once. A bottomless Mickey on a stage in Times Square.

There are five cars in the Danowitz driveway, including my mother's. It must be a holiday. I think there's a Jewish celebration of some kind on every single day of the Jewish calendar. Aside from the weekly ceremonies, Shabbat and Havdalah, there's Tisha be-Av and Lag ba-Omer and Asarah be-Tevet and Purim and of course the heavy hitters, Rosh Hashanah and Yom Kippur. Each one commemorates a mass slaughter of some degree in which the Jews of the time became too prosperous or joyous and wound up very dead. Today must be one of those days. I park about three houses down and start to feel the nervousness of my intentions. Ring the bell, ask where Miriam is, see her, say hi, say sorry, hand her the photo?

As I ring the bell my stomach drops and burns. Becca Danowitz sees me through the glass and cannot fake her utter disappointment. I can't tell if it's her impenetrable mean streak or just the lack of respect she holds behind her eyes, but she will forever look at me as if I've let the entire religion down with my ignorance, youth, and raw stupidity. It's there, even when she tries to smile, like she's doing right now as she opens the door. I can see the bottom row of her teeth and the raised mole that invades her right eyebrow.

"Hello, David. We weren't expecting you. I'll get your mother." Standing on the porch, I lean my head in and look for my sister. I see the *mechitzah* separating the men and women. This one's made of a heavy wood and has triangular holes cut into it.

"What are you doing?" my mother says, and she's there, at the door, with more shock on her face than pleasure.

"Hi, Mom."

"What are you doing here?"

"I came to see you."

She looks back into the house where Debra stares at me.

"David?" Debra says, and moves to me. I hold her with my eyes closed, so close to me. My mother is watching, waiting.

"This isn't a good time," my mother says. "We're having a celebration."

"Oh."

"Have you come to apologize?"

I tap the photo in my left pocket and know she's right. It isn't a good time. "I'm sorry, Mom."

"Well, just as I've told Dena, you *betrayed* me. That's how it feels. A betrayal of trust. Trust is earned. How are you going to earn it back?"

I see Peter Rabbi walking up behind her. He's about my height and has a black and gray beard that's wider than it is long. I feel some relief when a smile forms behind the hair on his face.

"Da*vee*d!" he says, opening the door and taking me by the shoulder. Just like that, I'm in the house and on the male side of the screen. I look back for my mother and sister and see them heading into the kitchen. The room is small and dimly lit. It has a low ceiling and a velvety, mustard colored couch covered in plastic. A swirly gold-framed portrait of the Grand Rabbi hangs above the fireplace. His beard is black in this one and he's young, a teenager maybe, grinning like a regular person you might know. Hundreds, maybe thousands of books are stacked on shelves and in milk crates pushed into the corners on the wood floor: *In the Land of Prayer, A Maimonides Reader, Fundamentals of the Rambam*. Two men in fedoras are on the couch. When they see me, they stand and one of them asks me if I'm Jewish. I nod and he asks me if I was bar mitzvahed. I shake my head and he asks if I lay tefillin?

"No," I say, and he wants to know if I'd like to do it now. "No," I say. "I'm just here to see my mother and sister."

The two of them speak in Yiddish for a moment and one asks, "Are you Miriam's son?"

"Yes."

They both smile and offer their hands. The taller one is called Yussi and the guy with all the questions is Svi. They sit back down and continue their discussion so close to each other that the brims of their hats overlap. They speak in both Yiddish and English. I think they're talking about a farm animal or a plowing animal and what to do if your animal kills another man's animal. Some Talmudic thing. Another man, older than Yussi and Svi, about thirty, with freckled skin and a red-haired version of the Hasidic beard, stands alone by the window. He grins at me and takes a sip from his glass.

"*Shalom aleikhem*, my name is Avram. Stolichnaya?" he says, holding up the bottle.

"No, thank you." I can see my mother through the *mechitzah*. She's talking to Becca and looking my way.

"Friend of Pinchus?" Avram says.

I shake my head. "Sorry. I don't speak Yiddish."

"No, no, Pinchus, Pinchus, the rabbi, Mr. Danowitz."

"Oh, Peter," I say, and Svi and Yussi both look up at me.

"We'll start in two minutes," Becca announces from the dining room.

I look for Debra through the wall but only see Sarah. She is taller and nicer and blonder and foxier than any *baalai teshuva* I've ever seen. When I wave to her, she waves back with a smile, a flirty smile. Svi and Yissi are standing now but still talking about the farm animal.

"Verse thirty-five," Yussi says. "A man's beast injures his neighbor's beast and it dies, they shall sell the animal and divide its price. They shall also divide the dead animal. So the lesson here is that because the ox had never shown any tendency toward harming any other livestock, the owner is only obligated to pay half the damages."

"Half?" says Svi. "No."

"It was an accident, a onetime thing. If the ox had previously gorged another ox or any other animal and the owner didn't slaughter it or, or, or, or . . . pen it up for doing so, then the owner bears full liability."

"So just lie," says Svi. "If your ox has gorged and gorges again, just say it's never happened before."

Avram laughs like this: *hut, hut, hut*. Like machine-gun fire. He holds his glass against his cheek.

"Give it a rest for a while, boys. Isn't your life about to change, young Svi?"

Svi smiles, nods, and pulls the brim of his hat lower.

"David," Debra says and I walk to the *mechitzah*. She puts her finger through the triangular cutouts. I hook my thumb over her pinkie and we laugh a little.

"I'm so glad to see you," I say.

"She's so mad about yesterday."

"I'm sorry. I shouldn't have brought you. It was a mistake. I was only thinking of Dad and what he'd want."

"Dena," my mother says, and our fingers come apart. "Over here now, please."

"It's time," Debra says. "Shaindee is about to announce she's a *kallah*."

"A what?" I say.

"A bride."

All of the women and Peter Rabbi come out of the kitchen and to the front hall. Yussi, Svi, and Avram all walk next to me. Shaindee, Sarah's older sister, is pretty like Sarah but already a snood, you can tell. It's all behind the eyes and the way she walks, like a waddling, wearisome duck. She sits on a folding chair in the center of the room. Sarah sits next to her and the rest of the family stands around them. Peter Rabbi says a prayer: "*Od Yishama B'arai Ye-*

huda U'vchutzos Yerushalayim, Kol Sason v'Kol Simcha, Kol Chatan v'Kol Kalah. Let it speedily be heard in the cities of Judah and in the streets of Jerusalem, the sound of joy and the sound of happiness, the sound of a bride and the sound of a groom."

Svi now walks around the *mechitzah* and he and Shaindee both stand together. I look at my mother and her eyes are tearing.

"Svi and I," says Shaindee, "wrote in to the grand rabbi last week."

My mother walks from her spot and is now behind Becca, who's begun to yelp softly in what I believe is Yiddish.

Shaindee takes a piece of paper from a pouch in her apron. "I'd like to read this to you. It's what I wrote to the grand rabbi last week."

To the honorable and holy, our master, our teacher, our rabbi,

My name is Shaindee Danowitz. Three years ago I saw you on the street in Brooklyn and you looked into my eyes before a man called your name and you looked away. Do you remember that? I have enclosed my picture in the hope that you might remember me. I know that you see many, many people each day and are so intelligent, wise, generous, giving, noble, selfless, and kind. I understand if you don't remember me or my face. I am writing you today to ask for your blessing. I would like to become a *kallah*. The man I'd like to marry goes by the name of Svi

Kutensky and he is a seller of fine jewelry in the diamond district of New York City, New York. I am the daughter of a *baal teshuva* rabbi named Pinchus Danowitz. His *shul,* Ohev Shalom, is located in Vincent, New Jersey. My mother is also a *BT* and her name is Becca Danowitz. Svi and I have obtained the blessing and approval of my parents. And although Svi's parents, Jules and Edith Kutensky, are conservative Jews who live in Maryland, they are very supportive of our union and know that we will build a true and everlasting Hasidic home. It would please us both to no end if you allowed us to marry and to form such a family. I hope you will call or write us soon. Please feel free to keep the picture.

Sincerely,
Shaindee Danowitz

"And?" says Avram. *Hut, hut, hut.*

"The office called the house two days later," says Shaindee.

"And?"

"And I am a *kallah*!"

The group surrounds them and the *mazel tovs* are said loudly and often as the women kiss each other and the men pummel Svi with aggressive back patting. Peter Rabbi yells, "Now we dance," and Svi and Yussi start pulling me by my elbow toward the living room. "No, thank you, no, no, no," I say, yanking my arm back. "No, really, no thank you, I don't dance."

"You'll like it, David," says Peter Rabbi. "It's a celebration. All the men must dance."

"It feels good," says Svi. "I promise."

I have to nearly throw my arm to get free of Svi's grip. "Enjoy yourselves, okay? I'm not a dancer."

"You must, David," says Peter Rabbi. "A *wedding* has been announced. My daughter's wedding and you are a guest in my home. All the men in this home must dance together in celebration. Please. Now. Come."

Svi has a record album, which he hands to Peter Rabbi and in seconds a fast and rockin' version of some Hebrew wedding song starts, "*Od Yishama B'arai Yehuda U'Vchutzos Yerushalayim* . . ." Svi approaches me again and takes hold of my wrist. I cannot fucking believe this. I look down at my arm and then through the *mechitzah,* back at my stripper/Hasidic mother, who isn't helping me at all.

"Just do a little," she says, and I'm taken, dragged, literally strong armed onto a pile of stale Lichtiger manhood. My God, a circle of bodies whose hands squeeze the shoulder of the guy next to him to form a sphere, a spinning wheel of black garb that attempts to keep up with the drums and horns of this fast moving song. And as I'm flung around and around it's like a nightmare, truly I'm stuck on some Hasidic carousel of sweat and vodka and Hebrew prayer. I can only see the *mechitzah* and not the faces that look through it as I'm whipped around the room. Faster and faster we climb, these seemingly sedentary men now airborne and feather light, whirling me round and round and all I can think about is what would happen if the Polaroid fell from my pocket. Avram has a monkey-wrench pinch on my already sore shoulder and it kills so I leap out of this fucked up situation by counting to three before diving out and nearly tripping on the sofa. But I'm out and on the other side of the *mechitzah*. All the woman glare at me like I just shot God and I take my mother's hand in mine. "I need to talk to you."

"Why are you pulling me?" she whispers.

"Go back and dance, David," says Becca.

"I don't want to dance. I want to talk to my mother. In private."

"When the song is over," Becca says.

"It's ended twice, it's just repeating now."

"When it's over, David," my mother says.

"No! *Now!*" I don't plan to say it that loud but it comes out in a shriek.

Peter Rabbi walks around the divide. "David!" he says. "What are you doing?"

"I told you I don't dance."

"May I talk to you in private, please?"

"No. You may *not*."

"Mom? Are you gonna talk to me? Huh? Mom?"

She stares at the dancers, the song repeating again. "I am celebrating, David. I don't want to do anything but celebrate this blessing."

I fling open the front door, leap from the top step to

the sidewalk, and run to the car, where I turn on the ignition and blast the radio. Then I yank out the keys and slam them on the dash. "Fuck *yoooooooou*! You lying, two fuckin' faced Hasidic wannabe *stripper*! You have to be fucking kidding *meeeeee*!"

A person is there, suddenly there, on the sidewalk, a coat wrapped around her. It's her. I do not know if she heard me. Her eyes are bloodshot but her mouth shows fury for the disruption on this day of days for the Danowitzes. I open the door and get out and walk to her.

"I told them I didn't dance, Mom."

"You were rude to the rabbi."

"I drove here to talk to you. I found something today and I wanted to talk about it." I reach for the Polaroid and put it in her hand. She takes it, glances at it. Her eyes widen before blinking, and then I see tears.

"Proud of yourself?" she says softly.

"What?"

She looks down at it again, then gives it back to me. "So what?" she says.

"You were a dancer?"

"And now I'm not."

We stand there, staring at each other and I can see that she despises me.

"I'm someone better," she whispers. She takes a long deep breath that has her face pointed up at the sky. "It was exciting for you," she says. "To come here today. To my friend's home. You found that. Or your father gave it to you and you couldn't wait to hand it to me. Couldn't contain the thrill of seeing me, of hurting me."

"No. This was in a box in the garage and—"

"You decided to come here, in front of my friends?"

"Mom?" I say and touch her arm.

She flinches. "I want you to leave." I see a tear jump from her eye. "I love you," she says and cries harder. "You're my son, David. But I want you to leave here. I want you to leave."

The feeling is in my bones and blood. A trickling of nerve endings that prickles my skin. She walks back on the sidewalk, then runs to Becca and Debra on the porch. I get in the car and drive past them, watching them crane their necks as I go. My sister raises her hand to wave and I instinctively do the same, but she can't see me. There's no way she saw me. My mother's tears are on my hand. Or maybe they're mine. I'm crying, just here alone, driving and moaning like an idiot, like an actor in a movie, weeping as he goes, somewhere, nowhere, back to my father.

THE DANCER IS an Asian burlesque performer and she's dipping her big toe into a five-foot martini glass. It's a larger crowd than I've ever seen around the main stage. The music is live, a three-piece band with a drummer, a sax player, and a piano that's tucked in the corner off stage right. I don't see my father or Brandi or Leo, but Jocko is tending bar. I ask him where my dad is and he points to the ceiling. Up the stairs, I go. Brandi's in the dressing room across from my dad's office. There are five or so girls in there, all sitting and smoking and listening to her as she applies something to her face.

"Sleek here with elongated high arches. Shave them if you're a diehard but pencil and some patience is better. The rest is the same as before. Your face should be a creamy pale ivory with rose-toned cream blush applied to the cheeks with powder. If none of you . . . David!" She walks over to kiss me on the cheek. "Where'd you go, your dad is worried?"

"I was in Jersey."

"Go see him. There's pizza in the office. Pepperoni and mushroom."

Across the hall, I open the door.

"Fuck off, Bobby. I've been bookin' acts in Atlantic City as long as there's *been* an Atlantic City."

My father waves me over to him, puts his hand over the phone. "Where ya been?"

I remove the picture from my pocket and place it in front of him on the desk. In the silence that follows, I look out the window toward Broadway. I've noticed this before but if I lean the top half of my body outside, I can see the enormous neon penis that hangs off the Marion Theatre. Within a few seconds it will fire those thousand tiny bits of white confetti into the air. I lift my Nikon and wait for it to snow in May. Three, two, one, *boom*, there it goes. *Click. Click. Click.* I feel my father's hands on my arm.

"You're gonna fall," he says.

Click.

5. *Smashed Staircase Railing*
4. *Old Man with Hand in Garbage Can*

"David?"

3. *The Hasid and the Stripper*
2. *Burnt Orange Sun Setting between Skyscrapers*
1. *It's Snowing on Broadway in May*

"I guess we should talk," my father says.

I come in out of the window and stand with him, his hands on my shoulders.

"Ask me questions," he says. The band finishes downstairs and lazy applause is heard. "Ask me anything."

I put my camera on his desk before opening the top of the pizza box. "Mushroom. Can I have some?"

Part II

Summer 1975

Uncle Bobo

By late May, spring fades in New York and I can't find a breeze anywhere. Summer will be early and hot, I can tell. In the shower I decide I'm in a jungle rainstorm near Tikal. It's a typhoon, really, a mass dumping from the sky that leaves me deaf to the world beyond the plummeting storm.

"Save some hot water," Brandi yells from outside the bathroom, and strangely I'm back from Guatemala. When I come out I see the French final in the manila envelope on my bed. This one is multiple choice and like the other exams I'll take it alone and unmonitored at the kitchen table. SPD is the category. "Split parent dwelling." The status is one of empathy, I think, and allows me to be trusted more than students whose parents still like each other.

1. Je ______ assez bien Paris, mais je ne ______ pas où habite le Président de la République.
   a. sais . . . connais
   b. sais . . . sais
   c. connais . . . sais
   d. connais . . . connais

I go with C.

2. J'ai rencontré Claudine et je ______ invitée à sortir ce soir.
   a. l'ai
   b. la ai
   c. lui ai
   d. l'y ai

A?

3. Réflexion d'un touriste: ______ Bordeaux les enfants parlent français!
   a. À
   b. Aux
   c. En
   d. Dans

I don't know, D.

4. Je voudrais que vous ______ à la maison avant minuit.
   a. soyez
   b. serez

c. êtes
d. être

I think these are all fine.

5. X: Quand vas-tu voir tes amis de Grenoble?
 Y: Je vais dîner avec ______ ce soir.
 a. elles
 b. leurs
 c. ils
 d. eux

No idea.

I'm late. I decide to finish later and hurry to get to Larry's by two o'clock. His store is gutted; the chipped linoleum floor is covered in dust. He's got everything in boxes, including sixteen film canisters of porn movies that were never part of the deal. He says he has to get rid of them so he'll "give" them to me—long pause—for five hundred even. I tell him I'll talk to my dad, but I doubt it. He asks me how much I think it'll be to buy porn from LA or San Francisco. "This is a steal," he says.

I suggest he throws them in for free since he won't have much use for them in Boca Raton. Ole Larry shakes his head and runs his finger over the canisters.

"Ten each," he says.

"Deal," I say, like I'm Monty Hall. Though I haven't watched the movies, I'm pretty sure they're fine. Girls with no clothes on. People fucking. I'm sure they're fine. For the next three hours, Larry reads off his inventory as I tag everything in the store with product markers. The dildos take the longest: "The Great American, $15.00. The Squirter, $10.50. The Challenge, $15.00. Five-inch balls, $9.50. White realistic, $10.00. Black realistic, $18.00. Willy, an even $10. Knobby Ed, $9.50. Uncle Bobo, $15.00. Cock nose with headgear, $20.00. King Kong Dong . . ."

TUESDAY MORNING IS graduation. My father wakes me with another new camera. It's a Graflex, a Crown Graphic 4x5 with an Ektar 127mm f/4.7 lens. He puts it in my hands before I even open my eyes and it's beautiful and thoughtful. "Got it for dirt cheap," he says, and I hear Brandi in the hallway, "It's from me too."

"I love it," I say, and when she pokes her head in, I think of my mother and whether she knows what day it is. If I call her, she'll say, right, right, I'm so sorry and tell me it's some Jewish holiday like Erev Stinchus Pinchus. I'll tell her she's a better stripper than a mother, a better liar than a Hasid. Yeah. That'll make her love me.

"It's called a Graflex," my father says. "I put film in it. Black and white."

The phone rings the loudest in the kitchen.

"Hello?" I hear Brandi say as I get out of bed.

"I think you should bring it to Atlantic City."

"David, it's your mom."

"It's your mother," my father repeats, his hands on my shoulders. "Get Deb for Friday. Don't mention the beach.

Just tell her we'll meet her at Halfway Hojo's. Tell her it's for my birthday."

I lift the phone in my father's room. "Hello?"

"Hi. Happy graduation."

"Yeah."

"I didn't know if you were going to the ceremony."

"No."

"I didn't think you'd want to." Silence. "I mean . . . if you were going, I'd go but knowing you, I thought you'd think it was . . ."

"A waste of time."

"Yes. Knowing you."

"Yeah."

"How are you going to get your diploma?"

"They'll mail it. Where were you? I called you twenty times last week."

"We're not here a lot, David."

"You should get one of those machines."

"They're expensive. Plus, I hate the phone."

"But I can't reach you."

"I know, I know, I can't believe how busy I am these days."

Silence.

"Is Debra there?"

"No."

"Where is she?"

"School."

"It's Sunday."

"They're having a—"

"Will you tell her to call me?"

"Yes. Yes I will."

"Did she get my letter?"

"I don't know. I can ask her."

"Ask about Debra," my father whispers. "Two nights. Next Friday. Tell her I'll have her back on Sunday."

"I just wanted to say congratulations," she says. "You did it. You made it through. I'd like to send you something if it's okay."

"Oh. Sure, yeah. Listen, we're going to the beach next Friday," I say. "And Dad was wondering—"

My father's waving his arms at me, shaking his head. "You said *beach*."

"If Deb could come with us."

"I've told him this so many times, David. She doesn't have a bathing suit. And she burns just like me. You know how fast it happens. I'd prefer it if there was a different plan."

"That's the plan. She doesn't have to go in the water."

"But her skin . . ."

"Dad suggests we meet at the Howard Johnson's."

"The sun is very bad for the skin. I'll talk to him. Is he there?"

I hand my father the phone. He stares at it like it's a tarantula.

"Hey there, Mick," my father says. "Long time. Where ya been?"

Pause.

"Uh-huh, you real Jews have so much on your calendar."

Pause.

"I'm not being rude. I'm saying God likes you more. Keeps you busy. Makes it hard to see Debra."

Pause.

"No, no, no. Did he say beach? It's just a hotel."

Pause.

"But so what. Beach or no beach, I want to see my girl next weekend. We're heading off for my birthday. Big, expensive gifts only, please."

He's smiling from his joke, but his grin fades as soon as she speaks.

"I, I . . . don't care about any of that," he says. "I want to see her. I'll meet you at the diner or pick her up at the house. It's up to you. One weekend with her father. One! People do it all the time, Mick. It's what families do."

He faces me as she talks and talks and eventually he holds the phone away from his ear and points his fingers at it like a gun. "You done?" he asks. "Yes, I heard you loud and clear, Mickey. Friday's a school day. I just need her to miss a couple of hours so we can get on the road. How about two o'clock?"

Pause.

"I did listen to you and now I'm done. Give me a time, what? Two thirty?"

Pause.

"It's a couple of hours of school. She can miss two hours, Mick. And stop telling me she's too goddamn religious to wear a bathing suit. Do you have any idea how fucked up you're making that kid?"

More talk from her end and he ends up banging the receiver

against his hip. "*Excuse* me, can I say something? I'm finished with this conversation. Be ready to see me on Friday."

Pause.

"Good. What time? Just give me a time. Good . . . See you there. Tell her I have suntan lotion. Good-bye."

The plan is to meet at the same Howard Johnson's we used to go to during their many separations. Halfway Hojo's. I'm excited to see my sister. I haven't heard her voice in nearly a month. In my bedside table I find a letter she wrote me from the compound last year.

Dear David,

Long trip. We just got here. 12:30 a.m. Mom drove seven hours and thirty-three minutes and we only stopped twice to pee. The smell of this place reminds me so much of last year. It's a wood smell and also the trees around here, so big and so green. The girl in the bed next to me is snoring. When she breathes out it sounds like a whistle or a wheezing. When she breathes in it's more like a small motor or an old man. I am writing in the dark and can't see if my letters are on the line or not. It's like being blind, but I'm sure being blind is worse. This feels like the same cot I had last year. I scratched my name into the metal bed frame the night before I left but it's too dark to see right now. There is another girl in the room but I cannot hear her or see her. This is a new section of the girl's dorm that was built over the winter, along with a new synagogue and the boy's dorm. The building I'm in has ten three-person rooms and mine has a view of the Tree of Life, a huge cyprus that leans out over the outdoor sanctuary. I am thirsty. I'm back now and I have some water. I still feel the tingling in my legs from the drive. We got here and no one on the campus was awake except for Rabbi Fleeter who was in the recreation room playing foosball by himself. He looked very happy to see us and even asked about you. I hear so many crickets outside, like grains of sand on the beach, millions and millions of them rubbing their wings together at the same time. I am tired. I can't stay awake. Sarah should be here tomorrow morning. I like it here much better when she's here and I'm sad are dorms are different. The crickets don't sleep, I guess. They are like Rabbi Fleeter.

Brandi walks in my room with another present. "Open it," she says. Inside is a book of photographs by various photographers. On the cover is a black and white portrait of a woman looking longingly to her right. It's by an artist named Dorothea Lange.

"Thank you."

"Happy graduation!" Brandi says.

My father smokes his brains out in the doorway. "Hey, Mr. Graduate?" he asks.

Brandi takes the book from me. "Look at this page," she says, flipping to find it.

"Yeah?" I say.

"Tomorrow's Monday," he says.

I nod.

"Ready to go to work?"

JACKIE
$34.99
3/4 WIGS

Monday

AN ELECTRIC SAW CHEWS THROUGH a piece of wood in two-second bursts. It sounds like *reeee*! The bullet-fire hammering of small metal tacks goes on for hours. They use what's called a nail gun. *Wopboom! Wopboom!* The Imperial Theatre. Monday. I write it in the notebook. Day one. Pretty boring. Me and Jocko sit out in front and wait for the van to arrive from the Strap-a-Long. A regular who Leo calls Fat Albert saunters up to us and asks if we're open.

"Just the bar," I say, and steer him toward Broadway, to another strip joint. He heads off to the corner, scratches his butt for a second, and comes back. "Thought you were renovating," he says.

"We are," I tell him. "But the bar is open."

Within a half hour, each of the regulars is in their chosen seat, drinking through the sounds of table saws and drills and dust everywhere. Back inside for a break, I shoot three rolls and just know the pics will be filled with movement and story. One old guy that Leo dubbed Grandpa Munster wears the cutoff fingers of surgical gloves on his thumbs and index fingers. He says it's for counting cash. In this light his cheekbones form sallow, deep grooves that appear like hinges to his jaw. His girlfriend is an elderly ex-dancer named Babs. Every day she wears a black leotard that shows her bony ribs. When she kisses me hello—her idea—her breath and skin give off a mothball scent that triggers depressing thoughts in my brain. Couple that with the Dewars and Vicks and you've got Babs. My favorite shot of her is the one in which I caught her applying lipstick, in preparation of being photographed. The excitement in her eyes is raw, as if I just hired her to relive her past, to be the girl she once was. Liberace is in the picture too, helping her pick the right shade. He's a veteran of "Two Wars," who hardly speaks until his third shot of Sambuca. After that he brags about the "whores" he slept with the night before and usually asks Leo to smell his fingers. Merv Griffin is a very fat and pimply alcoholic in his early thirties who insists he's a nephew of Betty Gravel. Mr. Green Jeans has a purple skin disorder on his right cheek and ear and is constantly asking me if I've read novels I've never heard of. "What are you, a moron?" he says, glaring at me like I've been wasting my illiterate life away. Another man they call Rabbi—just Rabbi—wears a yarmulke and only comes in to drink beer in the morning. When Rabbi sees me today, he says, "Happy graduation," and gives me a long and boozy hug. Ira arrives and everybody stops talking.

"Where's your father?"

"Home."

"How'd it go with Abromowitz?"

"Fine. There are three filled trucks, but one is—"

"Good. Ya know your job for now?"

"Yeah."

"Then why are you in here?"

"Just talking to Babs."

"I need you out front. Where's your notebook?"

I show it to him.

"Good. Make sure all these assholes only take short smoke breaks and get back to work. Write it all down, names and times, in and out. *Capiche?*"

I nod and he grips my chin and wiggles it.

Brandi's "first baby"—the sex toy shop she's named the Sixty-Niner Diner—is being built directly into the walls of the lobby. Only three workers are here today and she's pissed off because there should be more. New everything arrives daily: carpet, lights, countertops, two hundred aluminum shelves—all just strewn all over the place. She tells me she sees order in the clutter and has an opinion about everything from the doorknobs to the toilet paper to how many pairs of crotchless panties she should order for Christmas. She's also rehearsing a new routine, which is why we're headed to Atlantic City on Friday. A femme fatale act, they call it. The Moraga Theater, two blocks from the beach. I've been taking pictures of Brandi's rehearsals with a choreographer named Etta, an eighty-year-old Jewish lady from Queens. Just picture a tiny wrinkly woman with a yellow ostrich-feather fan in her hand, sitting on a suspended moon that's fifty feet in the air.

I see Moses. 8:33 a.m.

I'm supposed to write it down.

The rest of the construction guys arrive too. 8:34 a.m.

Moses is the boss. He has a very photogenic head with perfectly stacked, meaty wrinkles on the back of his neck. He goes into the theater and comes back out a second later.

"Nothing is prepped," he says, looking like he wants to hurt me. 8:45 a.m. Leo shows up, thank God. They talk and head back inside.

9:29 a.m. The boys, nine of them, are taking a break.

They sit on the edge of the trailer and I can see the peep-show units behind them on pallets. Phone-booth-sized black paneling with huge copper hinges and large sheets of glass. Moses tells us that he's been installing peep windows all summer and is booked until Christmas. We learn ours is a "fuckload" better than the rickety "Textoil" unit at Show World, which requires ball bearings to lift the shade. Ours utilizes a new invention, a threaded "worm gear," that will only respond to customized tokens.

Dad arrives and Ira takes him to see Moses downstairs. A functional wine cellar in the fifties, the red-bricked basement has been cleared for nine custom built peep booths.

In each, a person will have an option to watch any of five pornographic films that will run in constant loop on a nine-inch screen. When the film ends it will automatically rewind and begin again. The music for the live peeps will be pumped all the way from Soundman Sal's turntable into two mounted speakers in the ceiling of each booth. The formation of this area is a circle of connected booths in which people can pay to lift their individual shade. The "reveal" is a twenty-by-thirty-foot "sex den" with a mechanical, spinning mattress in the center. Moses says this section of the wine cellar may be too small for nine peep windows. Dad says make less. Ira says make it fit. Moses says he can make a horseshoe out of the shape and it might even buy him more room. Another problem: The mechanical mattress may not have enough power to rotate because of the limited wattage he's receiving from the electrical sockets. My father walks out as Moses scratches the wrinkles on the back of his neck.

1:30 p.m. Back at the bar, Babs is in a bad mood and cries for ten minutes while sipping her Dewar's. I think about consoling her but don't want her to get too attached—words of advice from Leo. The construction guys are punch-drunk right now and howling at anyone female on the sidewalk. "Here, chicky, chicky, chicky. Here, chicky Mama." Weird. Vern arrives. He's a quadriplegic who wears sunglasses inside even though he's not blind. When he sees all his friends at the bar he grins and Babs stops crying long enough to hug him and kiss his forehead. I take a picture of it. *Click.*

The phone rings in the lobby and, as I run to lift it, I want it to be my sister's voice.

"Happy graduation!" It's not her. It's Ira. He wants me to take promotional pictures of Brandi in Atlantic City. He says he'll give me more "film" work if I rise to the occasion. When I get off the phone I actually yell, "Yes!" and pump my fist like an idiot. I think of my mother and what she'd think of me now, getting paid to take pictures. Brandi and her super-gay friend Hart arrive. He's a tall black man who carries a Batman lunch box like a purse. Hart says none of the shelves in the store are mounted right and points to wiring in the exposed ceiling. Brandi says, "Fuck!" really loud. The last van from Abromowitz's inventory arrives. Dad and Ira step on the truck and I take a picture of the two of them. *Click*. Brandi has a paddle in her hand that says HURT ME on it backward. Jocko's got a pink dildo the size of a baguette and says, "Merry Christmas," before handing it to Brandi. She puts it to her ear like a phone. "Is that you, Mom?" she says, and Hart nearly wets himself laughing, his palm to his chest. "Mom, you there? I'm getting a bad connection. Ma! Ma! Maybe it's this giant, rubber penis in my ear. I'll call you back!" Funny lady. We unload the truck for the next two hours and I'm exhausted and want to go to bed. The peep windows are nearly finished we're told.

8:00 p.m. Moses is taking a break.

On the sidewalk out front a man punches a teenager then kicks him in the stomach when he's down. I don't know what makes people so vicious here. The heat maybe, the subway steam, the hobo piss and noise. Quiet is relative in the city and the human is certainly a varied beast. The kid who got kicked doesn't want any help.

10:50 p.m. Moses says the live peeps are up and running. The system hums louder than you'd think, but he says the music should drown it out. Tiki is on her knees, trying to make all the workers nuts as she flirts with taking her T-shirt off. She looks at me.

"David," she yells, lifting her top to show me her giant, sheet-white breasts. Yup, there they are again. I've seen them so many times now, I don't even care.

"David!" Brandi yells. "It's Debra! Your sister's on the phone!"

Hojo's

BRANDI AND TWO OTHER DANCERS are already at the hotel in Atlantic City. My dad and I will pick up Debra at the Howard Johnson's and meet them there afterward. My father says he's nauseous and I find him coughing his lungs out in his office. When he sees me, he's angry or frustrated or both and says to go help Leo, "Put the shit on the truck."

Leo and I load the van with all the costumes, wigs, and props. A brand-new six-foot brandy snifter needs to be removed from its coffin-size crate with a power drill. We then need to get it on a dolly and load it on the U-Haul. Once that's on we need to unhook the hundred-pound half-moon that's currently dangling over the main stage and somehow fit that on the truck too. It barely fits but we do eventually get the doors closed. Leo honks the tune to "Let's Go Mets" and is off for the beach without us.

My father's face is more green than white. He tries to appear okay but he's sweating and his body is hunched over. I decide to get him a ginger ale but he's gone when I return. An hour later he walks into the theater with a big wrapped box. Inside are roller skates for Debra, he tells me. "The boardwalk goes forever."

It takes about an hour with traffic to get to Halfway Hojo's. When I see the sign, the tower from the highway, I think of my mother's face and pray it will be smiling or grinning or glad to see me in some way. I envision our kitchen, so long ago, a scene like a dream where I'm small and she's laughing at something, something I've said. The reward in pleasing her marks my mind and memory for life. Her station wagon is in the parking lot when we pull in, sitting right next to a Greyhound bus. The faux wood doors and smashed left taillight can only be hers. My father carries the roller-skate box on top of his head and whistles—he never whistles. I see my mother alone, no Debra, at a booth right across from the pie carousel and cashier. She's wearing a dark brown handkerchief on her head and it looks like her actual hair underneath.

"Hi," I say. Her face is more guarded than pleased.

"Where the hell's Debra?" my father says.

My mother slides out. "At school. I wanted to see you alone first," she says.

"You gotta be fucking kidding me, Mickey. We had an agreement!"

Two people at the counter face my dad.

"*You* had an agreement. It's a Friday afternoon, Martin. I'm here to see David and to talk to both of you as *adults*. Can we do that? Can we sit here and talk . . . quietly?"

My father puts the box on the table and I hear his jaw pop. "She can't miss an hour of school? To see her *father*? You're the most manipulative person on the goddamn planet, do you know that? I did not drive an hour to see *you*. I came here to see my daughter and you're playing too many fuckin' games right now!"

A waitress in a light blue uniform and doily name tag puts her hands on my father's shoulder. She asks if there's a problem and he says, "No." We all sit but no one says anything.

"Let's start over," my mother finally says, and actually smiles. "The first thing I want to say is that . . . I know this must be hard for you."

"I've hired a lawyer," my father says. A lie.

My mother stares at him. I look down at my paper place mat and rip a hole in it with my thumbnail.

"I think that's a horrible mistake," she says.

"Yeah?" my dad says. "I'm sure you do."

"Maybe I should just say what I came here to say."

"Okay, say it. We're listening."

She tugs at the handkerchief on her head and takes a quick deep breath. "What I came here to say is not going to be easy for either of you."

It sounds like she's rehearsed this. She isn't looking at me. The booth is so cramped. I try to push the table, but it's bolted to the floor.

"Good morning," chirps the waitress. Her name tag reads Paula. "Who's ready for breakfast?"

"Nothing for me, thank you," my mother says.

"I need more time," my father says.

"How 'bout you?" she asks me.

"Nothing, thanks."

"Okay, I'll be back."

I stare down at the hole in my placemat and tear it more.

"I have decided to get married again."

My father looks at me, and then my mother does too.

"Married?" I say.

"Yes."

"Are you even divorced?" I ask.

"Yes," they say in unison.

My mother's forehead is sweating and she blinks a lot. "He is a Lichtiger, a widower. He has no children. We're going to ask the grand rabbi's permission next week."

"Next week?" I say.

"And," she says, "if all goes well, we'd like to move to Brooklyn."

My father nods, eyes wide. "Brooklyn? Is that it? Is that the news you said we weren't gonna like?"

"It means a new school for Dena. It means new friends, a new synogogue for us. There will be a lot of changes for her."

"Where do I sleep?" I say.

My mother looks down at her hands. "You can visit us," she says softly. "And I can visit you."

In the silence of the next seconds I am hurt, punched in the face. I begin to envy all the other conversations in earshot, the safe and simple ordering of "rye toast, please, not white."

My father begins to cough and search his pockets for a cigarette. "You had us drive out here so you could tell your son he can *visit* you in Brooklyn? Visit you, Mickey? Do you remember giving birth to this one, do you? I was there, I remember it. Look at him, he's your boy."

"And I love him," she says, a teary wobble to her voice. "I'd give everything I have and everything I am today if David would embrace the life I've found."

I've heard her say this so many times before. But it's been a while. How 'bout it? Join the sect and you could be sleeping in your own bed tonight.

"You mean he's got to turn Hasid, Mick? Is that what you really want? A whole world of Orthodox Jews."

"I want my son to understand me. I want him to respect who I am and who his sister has become."

"Don't worry, Mickey. *I'm* his father and I've always taught him to respect all shapes and sizes."

"Then why?" she says.

"Why what?"

"Why would a boy who respects me bring that picture to the Danowitzes' home on one of the most important days in their lives."

My father rolls his eyes and thumps the table. "You're still talking about that? You're the one who left it out there to be seen."

"I threw it away!"

"But that doesn't mean it didn't happen. I told him all about it, Mick, the way we met, the—"

"Why did you give it to him?"

"He found it on his own! You put it in with all the other pictures."

"I would never put that picture in one of those boxes."

"Mom! It was in there."

"Stop," she says, her eyes now frozen on me and tearing. "It doesn't matter. What matters is that you pointed it at me. So close to my friends."

"You had a secret and I—?"

"I need to keep it a private matter for the rest of my life. Tell me you'll never, *ever* tell your sister and—"

"Oh, Mickey, give the boy a break."

"Tell me you won't tell anyone!"

"I won't tell anyone," I say.

"Promise me!"

"Yes. Yes, Mom."

"Enough already. He said he wouldn't for Christ's sake."

My mother wipes her nose and eyes and sits up straight. "Now, I'm not saying you cannot see your sister. I'm saying that there will be times you can see her, privately, and there will be times when you cannot, can*not,* see her at all."

"Are you done?" my father says.

"I'm asking you to understand, Martin. We're not who we once were. We are completely different people."

"Is that right?"

"Do I look like the same person you married? The same person in that picture? Do you think Dena's the same?"

"You've worked very hard to be someone else. But I'm still me. I still love my girl."

"She is in love with her studies and she's become an interested, intelligent, and involved *baal teshuva* who many people . . ."

"I *just* want to see my *kid*! Look at me, Mick. I *get* to see her. I don't give a flying fuck about your status in the shtetl. I'm not so young anymore. Look at me. I piss eleven times at night. I have headaches and heart burn and I didn't drive an hour to hear you say that Debra's too Jewish to see us."

"Did you give David a job at the theater?"

"Yes. He needed a job."

"That's his career path?"

"Why not."

"In pornography."

"Pornography?"

"Whatever it is you do there," she says. "If it's associated with me or Debra—the talk, the gossip in the community, Martin—she'll never be able to marry a Lichtiger. I won't be able to marry either, Martin. Ever."

My father's hand is shaking as he wipes his forehead. No one speaks. He stands for a moment, then sits again. "You want us to hear that you're an extremely religious person.

You want to us to know that nobody is as connected to God as your team, the Lichtigers."

"That's not what I said."

"How in hell can anyone as close to God be as close-minded as you are? If the Almighty One, blessed be he, knew how you're treating your son, he'd never, ever like you."

"That's a horrific thing to say to me."

"And it's horrific what you're doing to this family."

"*You,*" she says pointing at him, "have no idea what it means to keep a family together!"

"And you're full of it, lady. I may be a scumbag in your eyes but I love my kids and I . . ."

Paula is back. "Are you ready to order?" she asks.

"No," my father says. "No we're not. We don't need to order. We're leaving. Let's go, David."

"Wait," I say. "Mom? Look at me."

"*Now,* David. Let's go."

I touch her shoulder but she doesn't face me.

"David!"

"You won't even look at me?"

"Go," she says. "Go with your father."

I stare at the top of her head before I walk from the booth to the door. I'm not breathing. My father barks to himself and starts coughing. Outside, he slams his hand on the top of his car and his cigarette package drops to the ground. As he leans for it, I watch his back arc and his head lower and *boom,* he vomits onto the pavement.

"Holy shit."

"I'm fine. I must have eaten something."

He coughs, pounds himself on the chest and pukes again.

"I'll go back in and get you some water."

"No, I don't want you to. I don't want your mother to know."

I look back at the restaurant and she's still inside, still in the booth. My father spits a few times and straightens up.

"Let's get out of here," he says, and I get in the car. "Check for tissues in the glove box." He wipes something off his lips with his hand. As I look for them, a deep chill comes upon me and it's fear, I think, that's raising the hairs of my arms. I find a few tissues and hand them to my father. His face is a chalky gray and he keeps clearing his throat. He coughs hard and I reach to pat the middle of his back.

"What should we do?" I say.

"It's passing," he says, and starts the car. "Let's go. Let's go get your sister."

"No. No. She's in school anyway."

"Who cares?"

He sees me shaking my head. "It's not a good idea."

"*One* weekend," he says. "One fuckin' weekend."

The Greyhound drives by us and changes gears for the highway. My father puts the car in drive and follows it. I see my mother stand from the booth as we pass. She bends, looking for our car, and starts walking toward the door.

עקב ובנו

Just for Fun

I REMEMBER ALL OF THE nineteen days I went to this place with my sister. A horror I could not wake up from. My building was across the street from hers and of course I was never permitted to visit the girls' section. It was my father who stopped it. He walked into my classroom and literally grabbed me out of there in the middle of prayers. I remember my feet leaving the floor as he ran with me, a silver-haired man in a red-checkered blazer, jogging the halls of the yeshiva, looking for the door.

We're silent as we approach the parking lot and I just know this is a horrible idea.

"I think *you* should get her," my father says.

I face him but he doesn't look at me. "No."

"Just say we're looking for Dena Arbus."

"To who?"

"Whoever's there."

"I'm not going in there."

"Look at me, I'll stand out too much," he says.

"We both will, Dad. Just say you're her father and you're here to pick her up early. Or let's just leave. This is stupid."

He glances over his shoulder at the building. "Fine," he says, and he's out of the car.

As the minutes pass, I envision a siren and then two long-bearded men dragging him by his armpits to the exit. Or my mother pulling in the driveway to a screech, running past me, holding her handkerchief on her head as she bolts to the door. I crane my neck to see if I can see him. Two teenage girls walk out of the building and see me there, sitting in the tan Cadillac with the engine running. I may as well be an albino kangaroo the way they gawk and keep turning back to see me, a boy, wow, in our very own parking lot. They end up joining three other girls on the swing set of a kiddie playground outside a separate entrance. I watch them tell their friends there's a member of the male species sitting in that car over there and all of them look over at me. I see Sarah Danowitz before she sees me. She's the only blonde Hasid I've ever seen. And by far the prettiest. My instinct is to hide, to keep the story away from her, to move over to the driver's seat and get the hell out of here. But my father is in there. I just hate all of this. And here comes Sarah, to the shock of the other girls. Right outside her school, she's squinting, the brave one, and walking closer and closer.

"David?"

"Hi."

"Are you looking for Dena?"

"No. Not really."

She looks back at the school before facing me again. "So why are you here?"

"My father is picking her up. It's a birthday thing."

"I get a ride from your mom on Thursdays, so I guess he'll need to drive me home too."

"But we're not going home."

"Oh."

"We're going to the beach."

"The beach?" she says, and laughs. "Dena? I don't think she has a bathing suit."

"Well, yeah, she probably won't swim."

One of the girls from the swing set yells something in Yiddish at us and laughs. All the others laugh too. Sarah smiles and sticks her middle finger up at them.

"I better go look for my dad."

Sarah nods. "The beach."

I turn the engine off and open the door. A few steps toward the school and I can't see anything inside because of the glare. I look back at Sarah, who's now sitting in the passenger seat. Great. I walk inside the school and there's a hum of distant voices. It smells like body odor but it's faint and sort of pleasant, the way gasoline is. The scent brings me back to those nineteen days I spent here. I am unseen until I pass a classroom where a girl Debra's age looks up from her book and notices me. She says something to her teacher and the woman pokes her head out the door.

"I'm looking for my sister. Her name is Dena Arbus."

The teacher seems tentative and disappears for a full minute. When I see her again, she walks past me to the staircase.

"Room three," she says pointing, a Russian accent. "Up the stairs and to the left."

I nod and then my father and sister are walking down the stairs. The woman speaks Yiddish to Debra and glares at my dad.

"*Mein tater vil mir frier efpikin frier,*" says Debra.

The teacher nods and tries to smile. "*Shalom.*"

All of us say it back to her and she heads off down the hall.

"Hello, Deb," I say. I get a fast hug and I kiss her but I can tell she's confused.

"You look different," she says, and laughs a little.

"Yeah?"

"Does Mom really know about this?"

I glance at my dad. "Oh, yeah. Didn't Dad tell you?"

"I told her," my father says, completely out of breath. "It was discussed at length, so let's get going, I got a surprise." He starts moving toward the front of the building and we follow him. She knows this is bull. I can see it in her face.

"Mom didn't say anything," she says.

"It's been planned since last weekend," my father says.

"My birthday present. I get to be with my daughter. Did you leave the car on, David?"

"Your birthday's next month," she says.

"But we're celebrating now."

We all get outside and Sarah is still in the car. My father stops cold when he sees her. "Who's the hell is that?"

"Sorry, Sarah," I say, and she puts her hands together in prayer.

"Please let me come. I want to come. My mother's fine with things like this. As long as there's a parent."

"Your mother would kill you," Debra says.

"And what about yours?" Sarah says.

"She gave me permission."

"Just drive," says Sarah.

"No, no way," my father says. "I can't just take you from school."

"I'll call my mother and tell her," Sarah says, and she jumps in the backseat.

"What is she doing?" my father says.

A car pulls into the driveway and my stomach drops. "Look, Dad, look," I say and a part of me wants it to be my mother. It's a blue station wagon that drives up to the swing sets. Four little girls in black come out of the building and walk through the playground to the car.

"You're Sarah, right?" my father says.

"Yes."

"Please get out, Sarah."

Another car comes into the driveway. It's my mother for a second but it's not. My father starts the engine. "Please, Mr. Arbus," Sarah says. "My mother lets me do whatever I want."

"Are you gonna get out or not?"

"No," she says.

I look behind me at Sarah. She shrugs her shoulders and can't stop grinning like she just won a contest. My father starts to cough, cough, cough, and it looks like he's getting punched in the stomach. He reaches to roll his window down.

"We shouldn't do this," I whisper.

He snorts, spits, and fires a loogy but it's mostly on the glass. "Goddamn it," he says, trying to wipe it with his thumb. Another car, this one's green.

"That's the most disgusting thing I've ever seen," my sister says. I laugh. It triggers a sort of hysteria in me and I'm laughing so hard. My father looks at me, still trapped in the mess.

"Yes," he says. "It's true. I am disgusting. Now let's go to the fuckin' beach."

Atlantic City

I WAS SEVEN THE LAST time I stood on this boardwalk. I remember my mother in a man's shirt and a green ribbon that hung from her beach hat. I remember the taste of Fresca. But that's about it. The beach is long, about a hundred feet until the water, and there are swimmers and rafters on this hazy, sticky-hot day. On the sand are lifeguard stands and various patches of water from when the tide was higher. The amount of sky and space is what I notice most. And the waves that crash so far off the shore.

My father is very quiet and doesn't look well. The girls go in and out of giddiness, knowing, perhaps, how this awful crime will unfold. In my mind I'm unconnected from the decision to steal them from their yeshiva. I told him fifteen times we should bring Sarah back. "They'll figure it out," he said, and just kept going.

I watch the girls lean over the boardwalk railing in their matching dark dresses. *He can be a savior,* is my thought. A Robin Hood instead. He plucked them from God's arms and brought them to the beach, where the salty air fills their lungs with life. My eye goes to the symmetry of their bodies and the contrast of black clothes on blue sky. By the time I get my camera out, Sarah is removing her shoes and now her tights. In court I'll swear this was never my idea. I'll apologize to my mother, to Becca Danowitz, to Peter Rabbi, to the grand rabbi and to every sect in every Hasidic community. In Yiddish. I lift my Graflex and try to capture the size of it all.

"Gorgeous, right?" my father says. "Look at the water."

"Is this the hotel?" Debra asks.

"Yes, right here. The Swan. But we have time before checking in. You girls are free to run around. Take some layers off if you want. I'll go look for Brandi and see if she's got some suits for you."

"Out by the water," Sarah says. "Let's walk out there."

Debra pulls her black sleeves up past her elbows. "I think I'll stay here," she says.

"I'll hold your shoes," I tell her. "Go. Go on out there."

"Come on, Dena," Sarah says, and is off, down the stairs and out on the sand where she stares down at her feet in quiet amazement. Camera to my face, I hear my own breathing as I watch her kick the sand. *Click.* My sister appears slowly in the bottom right of my lens. Shoes on.

Sarah is running now and I have them both in my view. *Click.*

"David."

My father is hunched over and his cheeks are a greenish gray.

"Again?" I say.

He clears his throat and coughs like he's never going to stop. "I don't see Arlene. I need to go lie down. If you see her, don't tell her I'm sick. And she definitely doesn't need to know about—"

"Doesn't need to know about what?" she says, right behind us.

"There you are. Great. Good. When'd you get here, baby?"

"You're coughin' like a madman, Marty. Have another cigarette. Doesn't need to know about what?"

Brandi's in a long red wig and a white one-piece bathing suit and heels. She pushes a huge pair of sunglasses higher on her nose and steps closer to my father. "Doesn't need to know about . . . ?"

"I wasn't even talkin' about you, Arlene. I talked to Sheehan and we're all set. You're tight-lacing tonight. You know that?"

"No. No one told me that."

"He's a corset man. Eighteen inches, it's in the contract."

"I'm thirty-six years old, Marty. If Sheehan wants eighteen inches, he can cram 'em up his ass."

"And there's an interview."

"With who?"

"The *Peep Show Express*. Some guy over there says he wants to meet you. Just plug the theater and tell him you need to get dressed. Do not mention my name."

"Where's Deb?"

I point to the beach and she walks closer to the railing. Debra's sitting with her arms wrapped around her knees, as Sarah dips her toe in the water. "Mickey let her bring a friend?"

"Well, sure," my father says, and looks at me.

I will not be the person to tell Brandi the truth. My father barks out a cough and suppresses it with his fist. I wait for him to hurl right here on the boardwalk.

"What's going on with you?" Brandi says.

"Nothing."

"You feel all right?"

"Feel perfect. Look at my girl on the beach. Go tell her to take her shoes off."

Brandi looks out at them again. "I want to see her," she says, taking off her own shoes. I follow her down the stairs to the sand. When we reach the girls, Brandi hugs my sister before greeting Sarah. "No shoes allowed," she says, and Debra slips them off. I lift my camera and she screams, "Don't!" with her head turned away.

"Okay. I won't." I lower it and wait for her to face me.

"I think you should come home," she says. She scoops sand into her hand and we both watch it pour through her fingers. "I want you to come home."

Brandi slaps me on the head way too hard and says, "You're *it*!" before running around us with her heels dangling from her finger. "Come on, get me, David."

I hadn't realized how much I needed to hear those words: *I want you to come home.*

"Come on, slow poke," says Brandi. "Think you can catch me?"

I look down at my sister.

"Please," she says.

"Dare me to go in?" says Sarah, pointing at the ocean.

We both watch her lift her dress above her knees. She laughs and starts to dance, a Hasid doing the Charleston.

"I dare you," Brandi yells.

Sarah sprints straight for the water. The second her toe goes in, her arms go up, and she shrieks before running back to us.

"Told you it was cold," Brandi says.

"I think about you a lot," I say, looking out at the sea.

"I think about you more," she says.

"Did you get my letter?" I ask.

"No."

"No?"

"Where did you send it?"

"To the house."

"Maybe she tore it up."

"She's not like that, David."

"Then where is it?"

"I don't know."

"She wishes I didn't exist."

"She wishes you'd come home too," she says.

"No," I say, and have to smirk.

"Yes."

"Are you kidding me?"

"You have this idea that she's this crazy Orthodox lady with a prayer book in her hand all day."

"Yes. That's right."

Sarah runs past us and tags Brandi. "You're it!"

"No, David's it," she says.

I nod and touch my sister on her knee. "You're it."

She touches my shoulder with hers. "No, you're it," she says, and is up and running.

"I'll hold your camera," Brandi says. "Go chase your sister. I think she could use it."

I give her the Graflex. It takes me a while to catch and tackle my sister. I toss a little sand in her hair and she screams like girls do in horror movies.

"Okay, okay, I'm it, I'm *it,*" Debra says.

I tickle her armpit like I used to do when we were little and she laughs with her mouth wide and smacks my shoulder over and over.

"Where'd your father go?" Brandi calls to us. "Do you see him, David?"

I look back at the hotel. "No. Maybe our rooms are ready," I say, picturing him suddenly face down in the pool. "I'll be right back."

• • •

I FEEL BETTER WHEN the clerk says my father has gone up to our suite. I knock for some time before he opens the door. The second I see him he runs back to the bathroom.

"Dad?"

"Not now. I need to be alone."

"Is it any better?" I say.

In a few minutes I hear him flush. He shuffles out and collapses on the bed like a cut-down tree.

"Maybe we should find a doctor," I say.

He shakes his head and his eyes close.

"Maybe there's a hospital around here."

"Big night. Big, big night."

I run the back of my hand along his cheek, looking down at his eyebrows and dark long lashes.

"I'm worried," I whisper.

"I'm fine."

"About Mom."

"Oh."

"Should I call her?"

The key jiggles in the door before it swings open.

"Hello?" Brandi says, followed by the girls. My father sits up quickly and pats down his hair.

"How is it out there?" he says, trying hard to look healthy.

"Humid," she says, removing her sunglasses to focus on him. "Marty, you look terrible."

"No, no, I feel a little dizzy but I'm sure it's just the heat. I don't know. Must be the heat. You got suits for the girls?"

"Yup, yup, you ready, girls?"

Sarah moves directly to the window and looks up at the sky.

"You don't feel well, Dad?" Debra says.

"Feel fine, honey."

"The pool is big," Sarah says. "Come look, Dena."

"Let's go in the other room, girls. I'll show you my stuff and you can decide."

"Arlene," my father says.

"What?"

"You need to call Ira and ask him what time you need to be at the Moraga. And get Leo on the phone too. I have no idea where the interview is happening. And you're tight-lacing so . . ."

"I know, Marty, you told me."

"I'm telling you again."

The girls follow her into the adjoining room. When they're gone my father rolls over to face me. "Maybe you should call your mother," he whispers. "Just call the house and if she picks up just keep saying 'One night . . . He *deserves* one night.' Tell her I have the friend and I'll have 'em both back in the morning, as early as she wants." The phone rings and he startles up, stares at it. "You get it," he tells me.

The butterflies light a fire in my stomach. It's her, I know it. I walk to the phone, rest my hand on the receiver. My turn to puke. I lift it, waiting for her voice.

"Hello?" It's Jocko. I give the phone to my father.

"Yeah? No . . . who . . . who's late? . . . Ten minutes ago . . . What do you mean? . . . No, I told you this twice. Don't be stupid today. Open the live peeps only, the side door, and that's it." He hangs up and shuts his eyes.

"Is everything okay?"

He waves me away. "Don't worry. We'll work it out. I just need to close my eyes."

I walk into the other room where Brandi's pulling corsets out of suitcases and looking for bathing suits. She holds the bottom half of a red bikini up to Sarah. "Are you both swimming?" she says.

"That's not a bathing suit."

"Sure it is."

Just the notion of Sarah putting it on is exciting.

"Fuckin' *scumbags*!" my father screams and we all look at his door. "Of course we'll fight it but Keefler's gonna try and make an example of me! Jocko? Are you there?"

Brandi rolls her eyes.

"Arlene!"

"I'll be back. There are two suits in there. I think the red will be better for you, Deb."

"As long as that cock smoker's got the reins, I'm fuckin' enemy number one!" my dad screams.

"Shhhhhh!" Brandi says, and shuts the door behind her.

In the moment I forget about my mother and the crime. Debra sits on the end of the bed and slowly pulls pieces of clothing from the suitcase. Black seamed stockings. Leather opera gloves. Bullet bras, garter belts, patent leather stilettos, a black veiled hat. Corsets, corsets, corsets.

"So Dad's in real estate," Debra says, and Sarah laughs.

"Sort of," I say.

"Does he make porno movies?" Sarah says, and covers her mouth to laugh. Debra looks at me and swallows, humiliated. She knows more than I thought.

"No. He owns a building in Times Square."

"It's a theater," Debra says.

"He also has a theater. He owns a few—"

"Girls take off their clothes," Debra says, picking at the seam in the bedspread.

Sarah lifts her dress above her knees again. "You mean like this? I can do it. How much does it pay?"

I feel my face getting hot. "Let's talk about something else."

She shimmies for a second and laughs. "It's easy. I want a job. Dancing for money?"

"Not hiring."

"Do *you* work there?" Sarah asks.

"Yes," Debra says, and our eyes meet.

"You see all those naked bodies every day?" says Sarah, a mischievous grin.

Brandi opens the door with a sigh and walks to the bed. I am relieved to see her.

"Okay, which of these do you like?" she asks, holding up two more bikinis.

"I think this one," Sarah says, taking the yellow one from Brandi.

"How big is your chest?"

Sarah laughs and looks at me. I pretend to adjust my camera.

"I don't know," she says, looking down at them. She takes the bikini into the bathroom and closes the door. Debra watches her go, her face filled with disbelief.

"You want one, Deb? I got the red."

"No, thank you."

"Maybe you can help me then. Eighteen inches?" Brandi says, holding a corset up to her body. "This is gonna be a joke. Will you help me?"

Debra looks at the corset and doesn't answer, so Brandi steps into the thing with her bathing suit still on. She yanks it up and over her giant breasts and it looks like she's stuck in an inner tube. I laugh a little and she sticks out her tongue.

"Hey, Peanut gallery. Buzz off if you think it's funny."

"Sorry."

"I basically need you to pull on the strings in the back as hard as you can. And don't worry about hurting me because I've done this a thousand times."

Debra's baffled. "You want me to . . . what?"

"Grab the laces."

Debra takes them in her hands and begins to tug. I lift my camera and see it all through my lens. *Click, click.*

"Stop, David!" she says.

"Just one more," I say.

"With both hands. No, sweetie, you really have to pull much harder."

"I don't think I'm strong enough," she says.

"Here," Brandi says, and lies facedown on the bed. "Now, stand on the bed and straddle me."

An image of my mother. She's in the car, racing on the highway toward Atlantic City with a police escort. Fifteen cars, sirens blaring, and she's behind them, praying, cursing, fuming, pressing the pedal through the floor of the wagon.

"One leg on either side of my hips," she says. "Now grab the laces with both hands and pull up with all your strength."

"I don't think I can."

"All your strength. Trust me, I'm fine."

Debra bends her knees and takes the laces. She pulls upward, a tug of war with the strings.

"And again. Up and hard, up and hard. Dat's a girl," Brandi says, sounding as if she's packed in a garbage compactor. "Keep going. Good. Keep going. Tighter, tighter. Okay, now, tie it off! Tie it off!"

Debra starts to tie it but her fingers are fumbling so she tries to get better footing but slips and plops down right onto Brandi's butt. Brandi starts to roar with laughter. Her whole body shakes and Debra is bouncing from it so she starts to giggle and it turns to hilarity for both of them and I'm seeing all this without my camera so I lift it, despite my sister. I just start shooting away and in the middle of it all, Sarah walks out in the yellow bikini. I lower the camera again, trying not to gawk at this body, this gorgeous and smooth-skinned girl with her hair down and her arms folded and her eyes so coy.

"Debra," Brandi yells. "Stop laughing or we'll have to start again!"

....

"I'm trying not to," Debra says.

"But you're sitting on my ass."

Debra is cackling like I haven't seen her do in years, it seems. She tries to take the strings and hold them in place. When someone knocks on the suite's door, I hear it but no one else does. It's her, I know it.

"Someone's at the door," I say, and everyone stops.

"Who's that knocking?" my father yells from the other room.

Brandi hops up so fast that Debra is thrown off and tumbles onto the floor.

"Jesus, are you okay?" Brandi asks.

"Yes," Debra says, trying to stand.

"Who is it?" Sarah says, running back into the bathroom. My sister joins her in there and they shut the door.

"Coming," Brandi says. As she unlocks the door, I feel my heart beating in my forehead.

It's Ira. In plaid shorts with socks and loafers. I take a deep breath and sit on the end of the bed. He looks miserable as he walks quickly into my father's room.

The girls come out of the bathroom after he's gone by and I see Sarah adjusting the bikini top while looking at herself in the mirror.

"David!" my father yells. I run in there. Ira's in a chair in the corner and my father's still horizontal on the bed.

"The films we got from Abromowitz are shit," my dad says. "Tell him, Ira."

"Black and white, too grainy to see, ugly goddam chicks

with zits on their asses. A death penalty prisoner couldn't beat off to these movies. They're useless, just like Larry Fuckin' Abromowitz. Useless!"

I know what my father is thinking. The deal will bite us. My first deal. My fault. He lies back down and shuts his eyes. "Fifteen grand on a system and we don't have any movies."

"That's why we need to make our own," Ira says. "Like Killowatt and Show World and Pinchy's. They all make their own."

"Make our own what?" I say.

"Porn!" he barks. "It's easy. You do some auditions, buy an 8mm camera, a mattress, and a fake houseplant and start shooting. Post it in the *Express*, ask a few of the undercard chicks if they'll fuck on film for fifty bucks. I don't know. I'm like your dad here, we don't know dick about porn movies. We come from vaudeville."

"We're not making movies," my father says. "I don't want that in my life. Either find out where to buy them or pull that fuckin' system out and get the money back. We'll survive on the live."

"I know exactly where to buy them," Ira says. "But as soon as you get in bed with the goombas, you never get free. You know that, Marty."

"No thugs," my father says. "I'd rather open a Dairy Queen."

"I can name ten places on the strip that make their own. Buy a camera and the mattress and you just saved ten K a year in distributor fees and around two hundred K to grease whichever goomba comes down the road. How 'bout you?" Ira turns to me.

"How about me, what?"

"You're a photographer, right? Can use a movie camera."

"That's it, Ira. Hire my kid to make your dirty movies."

Ira laughs. "I'm buying you a movie camera for your birthday."

"Could you get me some water?" my dad says.

I go to the bathroom and fill a cup. He drinks it like he's been crawling in the desert. In the other room I see Sarah at the vanity table.

"This one's especially for you," Brandi says to Debra, removing a wig from its Styrofoam head.

It's the color of tinsel. The strands are light and floaty and reflect off the wall.

"What do you think?" she says.

Debra smiles. "No thanks."

"Oh, just try it."

"It won't fit."

"Yes it will," she says, guiding her to the edge of the bed. She pulls out Debra's ponytail tie and starts pinning her hair on top of more hair until it's all off her neck. Brandi places the wig on Debra's head, tugging it down until she's satisfied and grinning and beaming like a proud parent.

"Amazing," I say.

Sarah says something in Yiddish and Debra laughs and adjusts the wig.

"Please let me take your picture."

Another knock on the door.

"Jesus Christ," calls Brandi. "Who is it now?"

No answer.

The girls both run into the bathroom and close the door.

"Who is it, please?"

Silence. Silence.

"I'm looking for Dena," a voice says. "I'm looking for my daughter. Her name is Dena."

I bolt into my father's room. He and Ira are both gone. "Dad," I yell in a whisper.

"What?" he says, from the bathroom.

"Dad, she's *here*!"

"Who?"

At the door my eyesight blurs as I reach for the doorknob. And there she is, out of breath, shoving my shoulder and rushing past me and into the room. "Where are they?"

"Mom, wait."

"Where are they?" I hear her say, and then Brandi's "Hello, Miriam."

My mother starts banging on the bathroom door.

"It's me!" she says, crying now, rattling the doorknob. "Open this up."

My father steps into the room. "Mickey? Look at me. Hey, Mickey, can you relax?"

"I've called the police, Martin," she says. "It's over. It's *over,* Dena!" she yells between the hinges. "Just open up. Please. Open this now."

....

We all hear the door unlock and the second Debra appears my mother slaps her with an open hand, below her right eye. From behind me I see Brandi lurch forward and grip the back of my mother's black dress. She swings her body out of the way and onto the carpet like Raggedy Ann. My mother tries to get up fast but Brandi stops her with her knee.

"Who do you think you are?" she says to my mother's face. "Don't you *ever* touch her again!"

My father's tries to unhinge Brandi's hand. "Let go, Arlene," he says. "Let go of her dress."

Debra runs over and kneels down to my mother. "I'm sorry. I'm sorry, Mama, I didn't know you were scared."

My mother rises, takes Debra's hand, and leads her toward the door. "Sarah!" she says, and Sarah emerges from the bathroom, covering herself with two towels.

"I need to get dressed," she says to my mother.

My mother glares at the towels and her bare shoulders beneath it. She faces me and then Brandi.

"You're going to jail," she says, nodding. "You're all going to jail."

"*Bull*shit!" my father says. "Pure bullshit. You want to ruin our fun, lady? Go ahead. Go fuck up the best day she's had in her life. You'll be hearing from my attorney, Mickey."

Sarah finds her dress and moves toward the bathroom.

"Hurry!" my mother yells at her.

"Give her a second to put her clothes on," Brandi says. "Give her some respect."

"*Respect*?" my mother screams, looking at Brandi in her corset. She practically shoves Debra into my father's room. I notice my sister's hair tie on one of the beds.

"You forgot this," I say to Debra, holding it out to her. My mother pushes Debra away from me. "Don't . . . come . . . near us."

"It's for her hair."

"Don't . . . come . . ."

"Fuck you." It's what comes from my mouth.

My mother stares deep into my eyes. "Thank you for destroying my week. Son." She grabs Debra's hand again and they walk down the hall to the elevators. My father and I follow them with Sarah.

"And it's sunny out too," my father says.

"You forgot your hair tie," I repeat, almost pleading as I offer it to Debra. My mother comes between us, her fingers splayed.

"Let him give her the thing, Mick."

"No!" she declares, and the elevator opens. The three of them get on. I follow them and cram the hair tie into Debra's hand. When I step back, I look only at my sister.

"I love you," I say.

The doors begin to close, then shut.

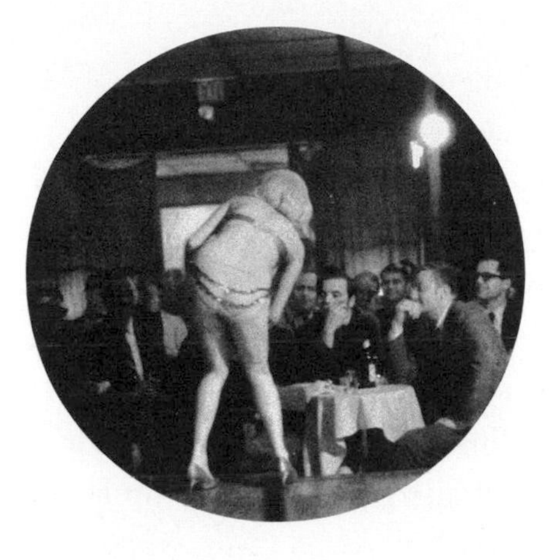

Get Me Home

GRIM. DEBRA USED TO WALK on her tiptoes. Tight Achilles tendons or calf muscles, we learned, made her walk like a ballerina in heels. A physical therapist with hairy gray armpits named Trina came to our house and told her to lift coins from the floor without bending her knees. It didn't help. She told my mother to massage the cartilage on Debra's heel by rolling it back and forth like a piece of Play-Doh every night before bed. That didn't help either. Why did I think of this in the first place? In the bathroom at the Moraga in Atlantic City there's a poster of a ballerina mouse. It's gray in a pink leotard and performing a plie. I try to remember what finally made her better. It might have just been time.

"David," my father says from the stall. "You still there?"

"Yes," I say.

"Is Brandi dressed?"

"She's waiting for the interviewer."

"But is she dressed?"

"I don't know."

"Will you go find out, please?"

An instrumental version of "Rikki Don't Lose That Number" is playing from a speaker in the ceiling. It's coming from a circle of a hundred holes.

My father flushes and I wait for him to come out. He looks awful and his zipper is open. "Go find out," he says.

"Are you okay?"

"Go."

Outside the bathroom there's a hallway that leads to dressing rooms, a small kitchen, and then the enormous stage. I gradually hear the audience—over two hundred paid we're told—and they're laughing at and applauding a Catskill clown named Willy Sapley. From my side view, I watch the guy hold his hat down on his head with both hands and run in a tight circle to loud thwacks of the drums. Then he's gone, diving off stage and throwing himself onto the laps of audience members. He climbs on the backs of their chairs, looks like he's swimming, as he takes a man's watch and rummages through a fat lady's purse.

"Hey, kid," someone says. "You know where Brandi Lady is? I'm supposed to do an interview."

The guy follows me to one of the dressing rooms and I knock. Brandi, in full fetish garb, opens the door. The corset, the nylons, the leather boots up to her thighs. Her hair is wound in a tall, blue-black beehive with thin wisps that fall over her shoulders. "Your interviewer is here," I tell her.

"Where's you father?"

"In the bathroom."

"Brandi Lady?"

She ignores the man and walks back to her vanity table. "Your mother did this to him. I just want you to know that. He's been doing better, taking his meds, trying to smoke less. He would have been fine but no, fuck no, she had to swoop down on her broomstick and just . . . kill all of it." I see her chin wrinkle up as she sniffs then carefully dabs her eye with a tissue. "I feel so sorry for you. And Debra."

"Brandi, this man is here for an interview."

"Yes, hello," she says.

"Hi, I'm Rich from the *Peep Show Express*. We met a long time ago in—"

"How long will this take? I have to be on stage in fifteen minutes."

"I'll make it fast. Do you mind if I record it?"

"No, but it has to be quick."

The guy puts a tape recorder on the table and connects a microphone. "Ready?"

"Sure," she says, facing the mirror, still applying makeup.

The man pushes Record. "*Peep Show Express*, June 1975. Brandi Lady interview. I first met Brandi Lady when her name was Luna Von at a convention in Sweden back in 1963. She was nineteen at the time and making her debut film, *Where Ya Puttin' That?* with director Rune Tharsz—"

"Wait, wait, wait," she interrupts.

In the reflection of the mirror, I watch her lower her head. Luna Von? Debut film?

"Is something wrong?" the man asks.

"I do not want to talk about that," she says.

"You mean the movies?"

Brandi swivels around in her chair. Her face is flushed and her eyes are on me. "Will you go check on your father, please?"

I nod and walk out of the room but the door stays open a crack.

"Go ahead," she says. "That's just my stepson."

"Oh, I'm sorry, I didn't know. Okay. Uh . . . we sit here today at the Tri-State Burlesque Review at the Moraga in Atlantic City where Brandi will take the stage in minutes."

"Hi, Brandi."

"Hi."

"Do you remember me?"

"No. And I hope you're here to ask me about the updated Imperial Theatre on Eighth Avenue and Broadway in Times Square, the greatest spot on earth for discreet adult mischief, including the brand-new and naughty toy store we call the Sixty-Niner Diner. Where everything you can imagine is for sale and *on* sale."

"The Imperial in Times Square. Okay. Is it possible to ask you a few questions about your earlier films?"

"I don't talk about that anymore because I don't make them anymore. What do you want to know?"

"You still have a fan base in Europe, a lot of people write in. Why'd you stop making them so long ago."

"Because I stopped wanting to fuck on film. How's that?"

"*David!*" my father says, and I jump back from the door. He and Ira walk toward me. "Where's Brandi?"

I point at her dressing room.

"Is she dressed?"

"No. I mean *yes*."

He opens the door a bit, pokes his head in.

"Almost done," I hear the interviewer say. "Now, in *Ouch Too Deep,* there was a scene where you and Bruce Girth had a standing sixty-nine scene on a cherry picker."

"That's not a question."

"Can you tell us a little about that scene?"

"Dwayne Shooter and Bruce Girth. They were veterans and I was a kid, well, we were all kids except Rune, who was more like a dad. We lived together in a house in Stockholm that had a garden and a pool and that's what we did there. We let Rune follow us around with his camera. I remember being very happy and knowing that no one at home would ever speak to me again. Mostly because I'd left high school. That was the big thing in my house. Love was always conditional, all of it, all dependent on God and order and keeping score."

"Darling?" my father says.

"Yes."

"It's time to go on."

"That's all the time I have," Brandi says.

"Okay, so three nights here at the Moraga for the Tri-State Burlesque Review and then what?"

"Back to the newly renovated Imperial Theatre on Eighth Avenue and Broadway where one can experience a true adult fantasy world where dreams of all kinds can be fulfilled in a clean and safe environment. I'm also performing a fetish act and a new act in which I bathe in a five-foot brandy snifter on Mondays and Fridays at eleven a.m., three p.m., and nine p.m. I begin a half-moon routine on September first but only at the nine p.m. show."

"Arlene!" my father says.

"I'm coming, Marty."

Ira pokes his head in the room. "How we doin' in here?"

"She's fine," my father says, "she's fine. Let's get to the stage, it's time."

We all walk down the hall and all I can think about is Brandi on a cherry picker in Stockholm. We haven't had eye contact since she came out.

"Don't just stand there," Ira says. "Take pictures."

Ira seems to know every dancer and manager we pass. I lift my camera as the curved, lit stage comes into view. Five women in fetish gear just like Brandi's are waiting by the curtain. *Click*.

Ira wants to introduce Brandi to a white-haired guy in billiard-ball suspenders. "Brandi Lady," he says, "Meet my old, dear friend, Alan Greenstein. Alan owns the Calabra and Mo Mo's and the old Groppler Theatre. We've been friends since we were boys."

Greenstein takes Brandi's hand and kisses her right leather glove. She curtsies as he does it. "You're lookin' at a headliner," Ira says. "A girl who's done it all and is still hot at, what now, honey, thirty-six?"

She puts her hands on her hips. "Do I look thirty-six?"

They both laugh with their mouths wide and Greenstein slowly kisses the other hand.

"Marty," says Ira, "you remember my friend, Alan Greenstein?"

"Yeah, of course, Greenstein. The last time I saw you, you were getting blown by some Asian teenager at the Exotic."

"*Marty,*" Brandi says.

"You still a fuckin' pedophile?"

Greenstein stares at my father as he walks past him toward the stage. Ira's embarrassed and tries to laugh it off. "Marty's been sick today."

"Go fuck yourself, Arbus," Greenstein says.

"Go kill yourself," my father says.

The day just keeps getting better from here. My dad guides me closer to the stage and points at Willy Sapley. The guy crams his hands in his clown pockets with his arms elbow deep.

"You just *shit* all over a great friend of mine," Ira says.

"Guy's a Nazi, Ira."

"*You're* the Nazi. You owe him an apology."

"Not gonna happen."

"He sends us dancers, he sends us clients, he's been on the fuckin' strip longer than you, Marty. Okay? Okay, tough guy?"

The lights go out and the curtain drops and the crowd is large and present, a lot of them. Willy Sapley jogs off the other side of the stage. My father kisses Brandi who now lines up with the other five dancers. "You go knock 'em dead now, okay?"

The girls all walk on stage and the set dressers push out six black chairs. Brandi is kneeling in the center of the stage with a bullwhip in her hand. She says something to the other women.

"You should go down front," my father says and I head toward the steps down. The music starts, a saxophone by itself, and the next thing I hear is a thud, bone on wood. As I turn I see him, my father, lying on his side with his eyes fluttering. The time it takes to run to him is forever in my mind. I roll him over and lift the back of his head. "Dad!"

"What happened?"

When I look up I see Alan Greenstein.

"Please, go get help. *Please!*"

"What's happened to him?" he says, his hand on his forehead.

"I don't know. *Dad?*"

Greenstein kneels next to me. He takes my father's face in his fingers and gives him a light shake. "Don't do it here, Arbus," he says. "Not in front of your kid. Come on . . . wake *up*!"

My father's eyes open. He swallows and looks in my eyes. "Get me home."

Adenomatous

THE DOCTOR IS A MAN Ira knows. We've woken him by our phone call but I don't feel bad because it's only eight thirty at night. I find the house about a mile from the Moraga, right next to a church. When we get there, the guy is on the porch in a bathrobe, waving his arms like a castaway. He gives my father a few pokes and checks his temperature. He says it's fatigue, the flu, bad food, an ulcer, or worse. He gives him a pink pill for acid reflux and something to drink and tells my dad he should spend the night. If he feels better tomorrow, we'll drive back to the city to "get the stomach scoped." He asks me if I'm staying and when I say yes, he tosses me a blanket and slowly clomps up his staircase. The room we're in has a TV and a phone and a mural of a zoo train with a rhinoceros in overalls. My father's eyes are closed so I lift the phone and call Leo at the theater. He's positive my dad is dying and wants directions. It takes almost two hours but he gets here and rings the bell and wakes up the doctor and his wife. Nine seconds later, Brandi and Ira ring the bell. Brandi, in a Little Bo Peep costume, leans in to kiss my father.

"Marty," she says. "I'm here. I'm here now."

"You can't all stay," the doctor says.

Ira hands him some cash but the doctor won't take it. "I'm going back to bed, Ira. Only one of you can stay. Please."

It's very hard for me to walk out of the place without my dad. But Leo and I listen to Brandi and decide to go back to the hotel. She stays. When we get there, I feel like I've been punched in the chest. Rubbing it doesn't help. Leo suggests we go home and I agree. In the car he tells me to take deep breaths and tries to put my seat back. I wish I could cry. The wheezing in my father's breath. The sound of his head on the floor.

"He's gonna be okay," Leo says. "Your dad's one of the toughest guy I know."

The rain on the windshield is light at first but soon the road grows slick beneath the tires. The wooshing sound is soothing somehow and I close my eyes.

"You want the radio on?" Leo says.

I shake my head and neither of us speaks for an hour or more. In the dream I see my dad and my mom on our front lawn. She's planting seeds with green rubber gloves and he's yelling at her, telling her she's doing it wrong. "I didn't drop out of my mother's bunny-hole yesterday," he yells. "I know how to swim! I know how to fuckin' swim!"

"Help me, Marty. Help me. I'm trying to get us there."

"You couldn't get us there if you tried, baby. You don't have the balls."

Leo has his hand on my elbow. "You're talking all crazy," he says with a smile.

"I am?"

"What are you dreaming about?"

Out the window the rain picks up. Leo's windshield wipers fight hard but seem fatigued by the quick back and forth.

"My parents. My mother."

"Did you know I lost my mom," Leo says. "She didn't make it to forty." A teacher, a churchgoer, a mother of five. But always a sick person, lying in bed with swollen fingers. A "disease" he calls it and I picture her there, under the quilts, medicine bottles and paper cups he brought her with bendy straws. I feel so much sorrow for him as we drive, envisioning this little boy, watching his mother from the hallway, waiting for her to die. By one thirty we're back and Leo drops me at my father's apartment. The sounds of the city are louder with no one there. And the loneliness I dread is in every corner. In bed I see Brandi on a cherry picker. My father in a grave. Debra in a tinseled wig. My mother on stage. A poem. Everyone's an animal and I watch through the cage. This dream's about a row boat but my mother's not there. It's Brandi. My father kisses the hard fabric on the front of her corset before jumping in the black lake water, pinching his nostrils. I wait for him to come up but he doesn't so I run to the edge and see the back of his head. The sweater he's wearing is wool and I grip the neck but it's too wet and heavy with soggy weight. I lift with all my strength. Please, please, help me. But I can't lift him out. The doorbell wakes me and the clock says 4:16 a.m. It's Brandi.

"Things got worse," she says. "He's over at Roosevelt Hospital."

THE DOCTOR IS a woman with a Dinah Shore haircut and a chart and an easel and one of those sticks you point with. She speaks to all of us but only looks at my father.

"An adenoma is a type of polyp that is premalignant. They start out as small nodules on the bowel wall and are usually the size of a match head unless they go undetected or ignored for too long, then they can develop a stalk like the one pictured here. What concerns me with yours is the time it's been permitted to grow so look here, see this? Your polyp is larger than these and is sitting in an area of diverticuli."

"Of what?" my dad says.

"This pocket here, see?"

"Is it cancer?" Brandi says.

"The biopsy will tell us all we need to know. But I do feel that you should prepare yourself for the possibility, owing to the size and placement."

"Ffffuck," my father says, and slaps the part of his stomach that betrayed him. Brandi sniffs twice and walks out of the room and into the hallway. I look at my dad and see tears in is eyes but instead of hugging him or crying with him, I lift a plastic watering can on the table and walk into the bathroom to fill it. I keep the water running hard and loud and see myself at my father's funeral. Standing there with Ira and Leo—and Harvey Corkman, at the cemetery, right next to his own father's grave.

"Hello?" my father says. "Arlene?"

"I'm here," I say. "I'll be right out."

"Where'd she go?"

"I'll go find her."

"No. Come out here. I could really use . . ."

"What? You could really use what, Dad?"

"A cigarette."

I smile at myself for a second and watch the corners of my mouth rise. But it's fleeting, of course.

"We better tell your sister."

J MEN'S SHOES
BALLY
AMERICAN
RESTAURANT

Ya Fe Na Ne

No one picks up the phone. I envision my mother sitting there, staring at it, boring a hole through the receiver while saying "We're not here" to Debra. "We're not here."

But I'll find her. It's no problem. I'll be the one to find her and tell her. He's in the hospital. Not sure what's wrong. But he needs you. He needs family. No one picks up the phone. Pick up the fucking phone.

By noon the next day I'm driving to the Danowitzes' house in Vincent. I pull up in front and across the street, a neighbor with *peyos* and a furry black hat stares at my every move. I wave to him but he doesn't wave back. There's a small, yipping dog on the lawn next to theirs and I don't think I've ever seen a Hasidic dog, or a Hasid with a dog. This one barks at me and I try to tell it to go kill itself in my mind but it doesn't seem to hear me. As I step closer to the porch, the dog moves closer to me. Shaindee, Sarah's sister, is at the door.

"Shut up, Kippy, just shut your stinkin' trap." Words from a girl in a *sheitel*. The dog turns around quietly and disappears.

"Can I help you?"

"I'm David."

"Oh. Hello," she says.

"Hello."

"Who is it, Shaindee?" A voice from beyond.

"It's David," she calls, and I hear footsteps.

"What are you doing here, David?" Becca asks, with the screen door closed.

"I'm looking for my sister."

"She's not here."

She's trying to smile. I can tell she doesn't know about yesterday.

"Isn't she with your mother?"

"No one picks up the phone over there and—"

"*Is ales git?*" the *peyos* guy asks, now standing in their driveway.

"Of course, Menachem," Becca says, "Of course, everything's fine."

Sarah is behind her mother. I can't see her face, just her elbow.

"If I hear anything, I'll call you," says Becca. "Let me have your number."

"Do you know where Dena is, Sarah?"

She emerges with her eyes on me. "She might be in Brooklyn."

Her hair is gone. Like a marine but a girl. A Hasidic girl. Just a fuzz a half inch off her head. Becca glances at her daughter's scalp with nauseous disdain.

"*Is ales git?*" the neighbor repeats behind me.

"Yes, Menachem. Everything is fine. You can go back home now."

"Where in Brooklyn?" I ask.

"Kingsford, probably," she says, touching her head.

"I need to find her," I say to Becca. "My father is sick. He's at Roosevelt Hospital. Can I please, please take Sarah to Brooklyn?"

Becca's eyes widen as she shakes her head. I can see the whole row of her bottom teeth. "Alone?"

Sarah says something in Yiddish and her mother responds in a higher, angrier voice.

Silence.

"If I hear from her, I'll tell her," Becca says.

"Can you write down some street names in Kingsford?" I say. "Some directions."

She's gone, off to find paper and pen, I hope. Sarah comes out toward the door.

"Like it?" she says. "I did it myself."

I see a birthmark behind her right ear, and think about Peter Rabbi.

"My dad's sick, Sarah."

"What happened?"

"I don't even know how bad it is. But I have to find her. Will you help me find her?"

She looks back into the house for her mother or sister. "I have an idea. Meet me at my school at one o'clock."

"Today."

"Yes. But not in the parking lot. On Posner Road. Across from the post office. It's one block away."

Becca is back. But she doesn't have anything to write with. It's the Sabbath. When I look at Sarah, she turns her back to her mother and begins.

"Do you know how to get to the Kingsford Bridge?" she asks.

"Not really," I say.

The dog begins to bark again, as if it's never seen either of us before. I sit down on the stoop and Sarah plops down next to me, her shoulder touching mine. Verboten 101. Menachem, the nosy neighbor, just stares us, gawking at Sarah's crew cut. He slowly lifts his arm to point and Becca moves us apart with her right shoe. "Asshole," Sarah whispers. I look up at her.

"From Manhattan," Sarah says. "You listening?"

SHE'S NOT ON Posner when I get there but then I see her, running toward me, between two trees, ducking now, as if she heard a gunshot. When she gets in she's out of breath and laughing. "We should go, I'm not sure if they saw me." I start to drive and she looks back at the school through the yard she came from.

"Did you just walk out?" I say.

"Recess," she says, rolling down the window. "Just get me back by four." She turns the radio on. Everybody is "kung fu fighting." She starts to dance to the music, her shoulders seesawing.

I reach over her knees to get my map from the glove box.

"You won't need that," she says, and when I face her, I am so close to her, so alone with her.

"I'll tell you how to go," she says. "Do you have any gum?"

"No."

"We should get some gum," she says, and puts her head out the window. She keeps it out there for most of the trip, just grinning as the wind blasts her face. When I need directions, she calls out the highway numbers as we approach them. "Route 46 to the L.I.E., to West Thirty-fourth Street to Twelfth Avenue to Route 27 to East Fifth Street and on into Brooklyn." The sidewalk, the street, all the stores are filled with people in black. I'm driving by a supermarket with Hebrew writing on the window, just a bridge away from Manhattan. Jewish book stores and kosher candy stores and an ad for toothpaste with Hebrew lettering. Two boys with *peyos* and yarmulkes play Wiffle ball on their driveway, just off the main strip. Moishe's Hardware has a sign that boasts of a *zumer* sale that'll "knock 10 percent off any gas-run leaf blower and any forty-gallon trash can," if you buy it before the end of *yuni*. The sign looks as if it were written by a child on the back of a large piece of cardboard. When we drive past the store, I see him, a little boy with *peyos* and *tzitzit*, sleeping in an easy chair. I see mostly women and children on the street and wonder if any of them know my sister.

"Where are the men?" I ask.

"In *shul*. They'll be done by four and you'll see them everywhere. Keep going straight and make a right at the light."

I was picturing more of a city but the side streets are almost as suburban as Newstead. I do see redbrick brownstones and cookie-cutter apartment buildings separated by narrow, overgrown driveways but it's quiet and the trees are lush with life right now.

I've seen ten girls who could have been Debra and we've been here five minutes. An elderly, bearded man in black stockings and what look like knickers, walks quickly down the street with a prayer book clenched against his chest.

"Can I see your hands?" Sarah says.

"My hands?"

"Yes." She takes my right hand in hers.

"You have a short life line." She runs her thumb down my palm.

"Oh yeah?"

"And this line here is for love." The tips of her middle

and pointer fingers walk down my hand until my wrist, and I start to get a boner.

"Oh, oh, wait, stop, stop the car," she says, and she's out and walking up to an apartment building. She speaks to a teenager on the grass, then jogs back to the car.

"She may be on this street. Just keep driving. That girl I just talked to," she says, "Tzivi's her name. She goes to the compound in Maine. She once told me that as soon as she graduates from yeshiva, she wants to become a prostitute."

Sarah laughs as she looks back at the girl. I keep my eyes on the road, don't even look at her.

"Her parents must be so pleased," I say.

"Look at my neck," she says.

When I face her, she unbuttons the top of her shirt and pulls it back, revealing her collarbone.

"I don't see anything."

"Come on, look." She taps a reddish circle on her skin, a few inches from her ear.

"What happened?" I ask.

She laughs again, mouth wide, and slaps me on the arm. "It's a hickey, dum-dum."

"Oh."

And there it is. She pushes her fingertips into it and it disappears for a second. Ryan is his name, a "nineteen-year-old," she tells me. "He helped me cut my hair." Poor Peter Rabbi. Oceans upon oceans of Orthodox Judaism just pumped for years into this girl's bloodstream and what happens? Some Irishman with an electric razor is sucking on her neck.

She laughs, slouched in her seat, still touching her wound. "Turn right," she says.

We drive past a yeshiva and it turns out to be a school for Lichtiger boys. I pull the car past the building and immediately see a familiar face. "I know that guy."

"You know *which* guy?"

"That guy. Right there, on the lawn."

"It's Yussi," she says. "He's been to my house a hundred times, don't pull over."

"I won't, I won't."

I drive up to the corner and make a right. "I have to ask him. Stay here," I say. I park, get out and run back to the school and up to the group of boys. They glare at me, all turning at the same time, to see the stranger on their sidewalk.

"We've met," is what I say. "Yussi? Right? We met at the Danowitzes?"

He steps closer to me, lightly bumping the shoulders of his peers as he approaches me.

"You're David," he says.

"That's right. That's right, I'm looking for my sister. Have you seen her?"

"No," he says, shaking his head. "I didn't know she was here."

"I was told Kingsford. They may be staying with someone."

"With who?"

"I wish I knew."

His eyes widen when he looks over my shoulder and I see all the boys doing the same. "I speak Yiddish," Sarah says, and I turn to see her. And just as they all hear a girl's voice, they look away in unison, like a flock of penguins. One of the boys says, "*Ya fe na ne*," and holds his heart.

"*Vart den ir numen is Devoria Arbus.*" Just Sarah speaking makes them roar and scatter, pounding each other on the backs. Yussi can't stop looking at her haircut.

I give him my phone number written on a paper scrap from my wallet and Sarah walks away toward town, as if she's not with me. In the car I drive around but don't see her. Fifteen minutes later I find her back near the school on the same street I parked on. She looks relieved.

"You should have just stayed in the car," I say.

"Some of them don't speak English," she says.

"Yussi does."

"How am I supposed to know? I don't talk to him."

"Now he's gonna go tell your parents you were with me, Sarah."

"I know, I know. Who cares?"

"I'm taking you back," I say.

"Do you want to find her or not?"

"And what if I find her, Sarah? What then? Whoever she's with will see you. My mother, for example."

"Okay, okay."

"Now Yussi knows. You should've waited."

"He's not a jerk like that."

"I'm taking you home."

"*You* don't have to be afraid, David. *I* do."

"I *am* afraid."

"What are you afraid of?"

"Of Hasids. Of getting caught with you in my car."

I drive back to Vincent before rush hour and we don't say a word the entire ride. I drop her off in the same spot and she's upset with me, pouting and slamming the door. I watch her walk back through the trees, ducking as she did earlier.

"Good-bye," I yell through the window, but she doesn't look back.

IN THE HOSPITAL my father, Brandi, and Leo are all listening to the doctor talk about chemotherapy. The mood afterward is depressing, even dire, as Brandi tries to rally the silent room with some cheer she knows. "B aggressive. B-E aggressive. B-E-A-G-G-R-E-S-S-I-V-E." My father seems comfortably giddy or on some drug, I don't know. He tells Leo and me to go home and we end up at a triple feature a few blocks from the Imperial. *Spawn of the Vampire: Daughters of Dracula* is first. Leo's so happy when he sees the marquee. He starts to tell me the plot and can't wait to get inside the movie theater. It turns out the film has started but we buy tickets anyway. The huge double balcony theater looks out on a gigantic movie screen. I lean over the railing. People are throwing popcorn and talking back to the actors. The movie itself is horrible. It looks like someone made it in his own backyard. Leo just roars at parts, especially those meant to be dramatic. The next movie is *Mother Juggs and Speed* and the third is a grind-house flick called *Eat, Fuck, Kill.* If escapism was the goal, I think it worked. But when the movies end, nothing's really been skirted and walking out of the theater and into the light of day makes me wish I were back in the dark.

The Imperial is empty when we get there, not a person in the audience and not a sole upstairs in the live-peeps booths. A girl named Lana is alone in the store with two customers and I watch as she attempts to sell them each a six-foot blow-up doll called Lu-Lu Lips. They both cackle as one of them puts his thumb inside her O-shaped mouth. A group of already drunk Japanese salary men walk in. Sal starts the music for them—"Love to Love You Baby"—and announces a new dancer. She looks much older than the others and swings a fluffy purple boa around her neck.

"Who hired that girl?" says Leo. *"Jocko?"*

Jocko walks down from the sound booth.

"Did you hire that old lady up there?" says Leo.

"Yeah," he says. "What's wrong with her?"

"She's *old.*"

"She's not old. She said she was thirty."

"She's a *hundred* and *six,* Jocko, look at her."

"David, Leo, Jocko," says Ira behind us. He's wearing a maroon Adidas jogging suit and brown loafers. "I'm calling a meeting. Now! Up in the office."

We all follow him upstairs and are greeted by two girls

on the couch. The person closest to me is a tall blond with sallow cheekbones and nothing on but a pearl-colored teddy and white boots. The other is a redhead with giant, basketball-shaped boobs in a torn mesh cat suit. She's eating from a bag of popcorn.

"What do you think?" says Ira, "Stars, right? Okay, Leo, David, Jocko, meet the girls who are gonna help us get things started." He faces the girls and they laugh and he laughs and when I look at Leo he's smiling and nodding and lifting a movie camera from behind the desk.

"What's your name?" Ira says.

"Auburn."

"Awburn?"

"Yeah."

"Ya danced on the strip before?"

"Yeah."

"Where?"

"The Exotic."

"The Exotic Circus?"

"Yeah."

"You ever do anything like this before?"

"No, but I wanna," she says, and laughs some more.

"Perfect," says Ira, "that's just what we're looking for."

Leo holds the camera out to me but I don't take it.

"I have to go," I tell him.

"What the hell are you talkin' about?" Ira says. "You're workin' tonight, right?"

"I don't feel well."

Leo hands the camera to Jocko. He hits the on button and starts to shoot Leo.

"Get that off me," Leo says, his giant palm held out. "Quit it, Jock!"

He points it at Ira next. A film of a man staring at me as he eats some prostitute's popcorn. "I need you tonight," Ira says. "You took off twice last week." When he sees the camera on him he tries to swallow quickly and grins like he's at a bar mitzvah. "Oh, hello, hello . . . aim it over there, at the girls. Girls, do your thing. The director is ready. Say *action,* David. Say *action*!"

"Action."

Jocko points the camera at the girls and they step closer to each other. Auburn drags the back of her hand across the other's breast. It is quiet in the room as all of us stand there, gawking. The girls start to kiss.

"Tell 'em what you want 'em to do," Ira says.

Silence.

"David."

"You do it," I say, and walk to the door.

"Hey!"

The girls stop and the blonde one wipes saliva from her lips. Ira walks over to me. "Your father gave you a chance, David, to do the deal with Abromowitz. Didn't he?"

I nod.

"Didn't he?"

"Yes."

"Who fucked it up? Right! *You* fucked it up. I got a

fifteen-thousand-dollar peep-show system and not one usable porn flick. Whose fault is *that*?"

"I know, I should've—"

"What do you got? Dildos, lots of 'em, that's what you got. How many you sold?" He's stares at me with rage in his eyes. "Forget that. What eighteen year old kid in his right mind turns this job down? The boy doesn't want to do it, Leo. Good. Fuck it."

The girls are both glaring at me.

"What are you, a faggot?"

"No."

"Good, I didn't think so. Now prove it and take the camera. You're the pro, remember?"

The phone rings on my father's desk and Ira lunges for it. "The Imperial . . . What? Yeah, yeah, here." He holds the phone out to me. "*Take* it. It's for you."

"Hello?"

"Is this David?"

"Yes."

"This is Yussi."

"Yes, yes, hello, thank you, thank you for calling."

"Leo? Bring your big ass over here and help me move the couch," says Ira.

"I talked to my friend."

"Does he know my sister?"

"Awburn, come here."

"Yes, but he had a question."

"And what's your name, honey?"

"Dot."

"What's the question?"

"He wanted to know if you were related by blood."

"Sit together over here and Leo, you stand here. Give me the camera. Where's the on button?"

"I'm her *brother.* I'm her real brother. Please tell me where she is."

"What is it that you want from them?"

"What did you say?"

"I'm wondering what you want from them."

"They're my mother and sister. They're my family, what do you mean, what do I *want* from them?"

"You work in a theater, David. Yes? A theater where?"

"Now, Awburn, I want it to start out like you're friends but you're mad at each other."

"What difference does that make? I'm asking you a favor."

"Say something like, 'Hey, why are you late?' and then slap her on the arm. Yeah, like that, not hard, you're friends but you're a little angry . . . Good."

"Try Kingsford."

"Kingsford? Okay. Where in Kingsford. Yussi? Hey! *Yussi?*" He's gone. I slam the phone and the receiver slips and crashes to the floor.

"What're you doing?" Ira says. He's on his back with the camera perched on his stomach. I walk past Leo and the whores and down the stairs. In the toy store I call my father's room at the hospital. No one picks up. The phone is right next to his bed but just rings and rings. Ira's on the stairs. "Come over here for a second," he says, so I hang up and run out of the theater and keep building up speed to Broadway, where I turn right and just tear ass through the maze of people and their blips of words and I'm able to run for blocks and blocks without the slightest thought of stopping because the human body is a remarkable machine that's controlled by billions of nerves and brain cells and I use them to see my mother's face in the scatter of my view and to smash my fist into Yussi's big-ass shnoz.

When I stop I can't catch my breath so I sit on a fire hydrant and watch myself die in the reflection of an OTB window. I hate my mother. I hate my mother for hating me. Tell yourself I'm not here, just pretend I'm not here and you'll be sure to find redemption, you bitch. I walk into the phone booth and call the hospital again. Brandi picks up.

"Hi, get over here."

"What? What happened?"

"Deb's here."

"What?"

"She's here. Debra's here. Get over here."

The hospital security won't let me up until someone in the room picks up the phone. Six rings, seven rings, and Brandi says, "Hello?"

When I walk in Brandi's standing with a nurse. And sitting there, next to my sleeping father, is the girl in black with long brown hair. And I am good in my heart and lungs and can taste a breeze of relief that I am no longer in this freefall alone. She's here, with me, just as she was on the beach. *I want you to come home, David.* I clap my hands as I approach her and Brandi and the nurse both *shhhush* me. Debra sees me and smiles but pulls her chair closer to my dad.

"May it be your will," she says softly, "my God and God of my fathers, to grant that he lie down in peace . . . and that he rise up in peace. Let not his thoughts upset him, nor evil dreams, nor sinful fancies. May my family ever be perfect in your sight. Grant him light, lest he sleep the sleep of death; for it is you who gives light to the eyes. Blessed are you, O Lord, whose majesty gives light to the whole world. *Shema Yisr'ael, Adonai Eloheinu, Adonai Echad.* Here O Israel, the Lord is our God, the Lord is one. *Baruch Shem Kavod Malchuso Laolam Vaed.* Blessed be the name of the glory of His kingdom forever and ever."

The room is silent. Brandi and the nurse both have their heads lowered. *May my family ever be perfect in your sight.*

"David," someone whispers from the door, and when I look I see my mother. My stomach rips with nervousness as I move toward her, trying to gage her mood in her eyes. I am vulnerable, I know, a child again as I lean into her. She puts her hands on my shoulders and pulls me close. I kiss her cheek. "I'm sorry. I'm so sorry. I'll come home, Mom. I just want to come home."

Three, four, five seconds of silence and she pulls away from the embrace. I remember her eyelids. The blinking. The subtle shaking of her head. No. And I know what it means. I've been to the compound. I've seen how families deal with this. Rabbi Neihardt would say it is not a dismissal of me. But more an acceptance of God and his reasoning. It comes from the fourth of Iyar in the Hebrew year 5751 when a rabbi told his congregant that a messiah would come and one day redeem all those Jews who'd believed that his arrival was imminent. This process would be called the Final Redemption. So it's not about love this time. Or even maternal obligation. It's about the coming of the messiah. It's about the completion of a third holy temple in Jerusalem. It's about the ingathering of the exiles of Israel. And it's about being redeemed in the eyes of Hashem.

My mother lowers her head and swipes at her nose. I can see the scalp of her *sheitel,* the flesh-colored netting.

"I want you to stay here," she says, facing the room. "I want you to take care of your father. You're a man now."

I, King David, see flashes of silver go by her face, her hair. I hear Brandi's voice inside the room, and the nurse walks out, with a grin to my mother. I, King David, see the blur of rage that's been trapped inside my head. I reach out my hand, clutch the bangs of the *sheitel,* and swipe it from her scalp. And I run with it, a game of keep-away, down the hall toward the elevator. I hear her footsteps before I see her and she grabs it back from my hand. Her face is from a dream, a horror show. There is no doubt that a murder has occurred. I did it. I am the one, the killer.

"Leave me to my life!" she says through her tears, and

the only thing left to do is run away, like the child I am. The elevator is open when I get there and a little boy stands next to a woman.

"Hi," he says to me.

Does your mother love you? Does she?

"Hi," the boy says again.

I, King David, look down at him as he points to the bend in his arm. "They took my blood," he says, and I look up at the lit numbers of floors above the door.

. . . 6 . . . 5 . . .

I'll come home, Mom. I'll come home.

"Mister?"

4 . . . 3 . . .

"Yes?" I say.

"My blood was in a tube," the boy says. "They took it from my arm."

Part III

1977

Two Years Later

THE PEEP SHOW EXPRESS

— JULY 1977—

It was Ricky Jacoby, an ex–water heater mechanic from Long Island who brought the art of looping porn films to Times Square in the late fifties. Jacoby managed a cigarette machine route in the Bronx and stumbled onto a warehouse of unused nickelodeon film projectors. He bought twelve of them for twenty dollars apiece and by the spring of 1960, a snowball of stag films could be found in any of twenty theaters on the strip. The *New York Times* reports that there are over two thousand film peep machines in New York today. But the advent of videotape recording and the remarkable leap in Betamax sales has forced theater owners to reinvent themselves. Rhino's, the End Up, Stinky's Review, and the Plow have all closed their peep windows this month for lack of token sales. The Imperial, Killowatt, the Exotic Circus and Show World are all shooting movies in-house and saving themselves the costs of buying and shipping from California. Show World owner Roger Pines dropped his cover charge, gives you five bucks worth of free tokens, and is selling walnut brownies in his lobby for a dollar. Killowatt, a theater that's been busted twice since last June owing to Office of Midtown Enforcement and Bella Abzug pressures, just put in a Gang Bang room that features a twenty-by-thirty-five-foot waterbed. And over at the Imperial, the "homemade" porn is more than slightly grainy but features a twenty-one-year-old blonde sensation named Tiki Nightly—in booths 3, 5, 9, and 12—who has an insatiable interest in devouring whatever cock slinger they've booked for the day. Each girl cast in an Imperial film is contracted to dance on the main stage for two weeks after her film premieres. Watch her movies, watch her live, pay for a lap dance and she'll sign a glossy. After that, head off to the obligatory toy store, the Sixty-Niner Diner, where Imperial owner Arbus's son, David, has hung dozens of Times Square–themed photographs on the walls. An actual museum inside a dildo shop. The night I was there, Tiki Nightly, Candy Appler, Veronica Saint James, and the Malaysian dominatrix "O," could all be seen on stage, thrilling the Imperial faithful. And for a finale, the legendary and still sultry burlesque queen Brandi Lady did a fetish act that was PG at best but wonderfully nostalgic.

The prognosticators say the peep show is dwindling, that in less than ten years every home in America will have a Betamax machine and every theater here will be quarantined for detonation. Keep up the good fight, you Kings of the Great White Way. They haven't won yet.

Sarah

THE JUNKIES AND FORTY-POUND PROSTITUTES are all in bad moods. I stopped a fistfight this week by pointing my camera at the two skeletons involved. The gaunt seem to soften when they think they're being discovered. The pictures are violent and blurred but are poetic somehow. I think they're good. Leo booked me a job at Show World today. The heat in the film studio above the stage must be near 110 degrees, and I have every window open I can find. The guy who meets me is a dwarf named Gary. He says I was mentioned in an article in some smut magazine and I feign disinterest.

"The *Peep Show Express,*" he says as he finds it and reads aloud. "'Where Imperial owner Arbus's son, David, has hung dozens of Times Square–themed photographs on the walls. An actual museum inside a dildo shop.'

"You're famous," he says.

The cover of the *Peep Show Express* is a picture of a girl in pigtails with an unpeeled banana deep inside her mouth. It's not *Life* but it's still a review. I take my Rolleiflex out of the bag and Gary says, "What's that?"

"What's what?"

"I thought you was shootin' film today," he says.

"Film? No. I shoot stills."

"You fuckin' kidding me? The couple I got came all the way from Philly."

Gary goes into a huff for a while and then leaves. The toilet flushes and I can hear the people he hired in the bathroom, laughing their asses off. Gary comes back two minutes later with a lit joint and offers me some. I take a tiny hit and hand it back.

"More?" he says.

"No. Thanks."

"So Leo says you fucked up last week at Jo Jo's loft. What happened?"

I stare at Gary as he sucks on the spleef. Every two-and-a-quarter-inch negative I printed came out blank and now Leo's telling this guy about it. A four hour day and not one penny for it. Dud film.

"It won't happen again."

I lift the camera and point it at him. *Click*. "See? Sounds good right."

"What do I know?" he says, patting it down. "Just don't leave me hangin'."

....

The toilet flushes again, and the bathroom door opens. The couple is a Korean girl and a white guy with sunken cheeks and wrists like twigs. I can see him right now, hoovering the hell out of a mound of cocaine on the sink. When he comes out he offers me some on the tip of a key. I tell him I'm already stoned.

"Let's do this," he screams, and in seconds I'm on one knee with my forehead way too close to his ass. I'm going to hell. Yuck. Jesus. At least the camera's firing well. BJ, doggy, sixty-nine, and a couple of "unusuals" because the coke fiend says he can blow himself.

"I just shoot hetero," I tell him, and he assures me, "There's nothin' homo about it."

On his back he flips up and over and yes, with his head and neck quivering to the goal, he does it, gets it in his mouth.

"Wow!" Gary says. "Shoot it, David, shoot."

Click.

The guy pulls his face off his wang and sort of pumps his fist. Gary claps and the girl throws her boyfriend a towel. Done.

I CAN ONLY smile in front the air conditioner at the next one. The crisp air is like snowfall on my face, my eyelids. The guy I meet is new and has the same brown shoes as me. The second I take out the Rolleiflex he tells me he prefers 35mm for his "rag." Luckily I have my Nikon and I load it just as the girl arrives. She looks Israeli but could be Italian, a brunette with green eyes and olive skin. The guy he hired is a marine, in for fleet week. He does a ton of pushups right in front of us before greasing up his pecs with some butter spray. When I tell him I'm ready, he's fatigued and sweaty and rubbing the butter stuff on his balls. "I need a minute," he tells us.

While he beats off in the corner, the girl and I talk about the huge antiporn rally the day before on Forty-second Street. I watched from across the street and thought I was about to see someone get killed. A woman who looked like Peppermint Patty threw a brick at the front glass window of the Raven and the bouncer on duty went nuts and started swinging an aluminum bat at her head. Peppermint P was tough, though, just picked up a bullhorn and screamed into the guy's face, "PORN IS THE SEXUALIZED SUBORDINATION OF WOMEN," until the cops arrived in and arrested them both.

The marine says he's ready and, although he's naked and out of breath, looks ready to storm Normandy. The Israeli girl takes off her robe and climbs up on the rented chopper. I aim the Nikon at her and she lifts her butt as high as she can.

Click.

5. *Livid Bouncer Wielding Baseball Bat*
4. *Peppermint Patty with Bullhorn*
3. *Tranny on Knees Kissing Sidewalk*
2. *Humidity + Heroin-Induced Fistfight*
1. *Israeli with Oiled Buttocks in Air (might be Italian)*

....

Missionary, BJ, cunnilingus, doggy, sixty-nine—and the marine hurries to his feet to finish. Done. I load black and white for the last five minutes. Silver chopper spokes, the Confederate flag. A military uniform the color of snow. Suddenly my camera moans and locks before it rewinds. I try to fix it but it's stubborn and just dead but we're done anyway. I run out of there and catch a cab to Cohen Camera on Thirty-third. The place is packed so I take my camera down to the basement to the darkroom and see the owner, a lady named Dorine with a bluish goiter on her neck. In the pure dark, hunched in a corner, I hear her open the back of the thing. "Film snapped," she says.

"Why? Fuck. Damn. Shit camera."

I take it from her and race to the next job, in the village, but the subway's slow, just putt-putting downtown. Leo arranged this one for me over a month ago, saying, "It's an orgy shoot, the easiest money, just take pictures of everything and everyone." I can't stand orgy gigs, though. The smell of ten people fucking makes me want to puke. Men's asses also make me sick. Going up and down for what seems like hours and the drone of the moaning, like a bunch of dying cows. Finally, the train arrives. I'm supposed to meet some guy Leo describes as a "four-hundred-pound dick with a blond afro and a cane."

I see him—no cane but a cigar—waiting for me on the sidewalk. A Jewish giant with drooping breasts and a perm the color of piss.

"Had to cancel the orgy," he says. "Couldn't get enough

people. But I got nine girls, all eighteen. What do you think?"

"Okay."

"It'll be a breeze, fast cash. Just shoot 'em standing there in their birthday suits. Think of the Rockettes but in the buff, right?

"Uh-huh."

"I say we do a pyramid. I say we do a football huddle, maybe a bunny hop . . . if there's time. See what I mean, kid?"

I nod, follow him up the elevator, and down a hallway toward the apartment. The girls are all in bathrobes and most are smoking. The windows behind them are huge and look out on a billboard for Christian radio.

"Line up, girls. He's here. Robes off, cigs out. What's with the pace? Wake up, he's here."

Some of them look younger than eighteen. I'm going straight to hell. I pull the Graflex out and shoot the girls, the billboard behind their heads. *Click.*

"Arm in arm," the guy says. "Let's start with arm in arm."

From the left: little nose, one eyebrow, blond hair. *Click.* Green eyes, birth mark on neck, blond, fare, freckles. None of these people are eighteen.

"Why isn't anyone smiling? I'm not paying you to look depressed. Ya want to be in magazines or what?"

The girls all push out smiles and stand with their shoulders back. The perm guy examines them and even touches one girl's hair, draping it over her shoulders. Scumbag. Or should I say scumbags. Both of us.

The fourth girl from the right I recognize, her eyes, her mouth . . . I hold the camera on her and she knows me too. Her hands clasped in front of her, she steps out of line, away from the others.

"Where the hell are you going?" the perm guy says, but she runs into the bathroom and shuts the door.

"Hey, miss!" he calls, waddling toward the door. "You better get your ass out here."

It's her. My God. The palm reader with the hickey on her neck. Peter Rabbi's *mishbucha*.

"Did you hear me in there?" he says.

"Stop!" I walk to the bathroom door. "Hi," I call, knocking lightly. "I'm leaving."

"What the fuck?"

"I know her."

"So what?"

"So I'm leaving."

"And what I do?"

"I'll call Leo if you want. He booked this for me."

"It's too late now. Don't be an asshole. I'm renting here."

"Do you have a camera?"

"If I had a fuckin' camera, I wouldn't need you. First you're late and now you're leaving? What the fuck?"

"I've known her since she was—"

"You don't have to pork her, just take her damn picture."

"She'll come out when I leave. Send her home and I'll come back tomorrow."

The guy gets in my face. His breath is best described as cigarettes, shit, and tomato soup. "Tomorrow? How 'bout this? Tell your father and that prick Leo that the next time I need the Imperial for anything, I'll kill myself instead. Got it? *Kill* myself!"

As I leave he gives me his chubby middle finger and calls me a faggot. My fight light goes off, blinking red, as I see him shuffle back toward the girls. I get outside and the city spins as I look straight up at the sky. I think of my sister at the compound, picking raspberries on a dirt path behind what's called the forest *shul*. She's trying not to crush them as she plucks them from the vine. "Help her," she says. "Help, her, David. Don't leave her up there." I walk back in the elevator and rest my thumb against the button. I'm sure she doesn't want to see me. But I open the door anyway.

"What the hell do you want?" the guy barks.

"The girl in the bathroom. I need to talk her."

His arm cocks back and although I see it coming it's a wreck I can't avoid. A meaty closed fist connects with my nose, the left side of my mouth. Specks of white dot the darkness and I'm on my knees, touching my mouth, a child in the schoolyard with blood on my lips. I hear the door slam closed and I kick it twice with my right foot. Forget it. I take the stairs down. I can feel my lip is bruised and swollen. I think my teeth are all in the same place but my left nostril is throbbing. Outside I head uptown, my lip expanding with each step. It stings when I touch it with my tongue. I think about calling Leo and telling him what happened. Fuck it. I'm fine, really okay, and decide to go to the next job. But if I see one single Hasid I'm leaving. Sarah Danowitz. What a nightmare.

It takes a half hour to get to my next job at some pervert's house in Hell's Kitchen, about a block from the Lincoln Tunnel. Leo says this guy works for *Doggy Style* magazine and pays double the going rate. I smell man-ass the second I walk in. Paunch-stomached, hairy people with floating comb-overs and brown socks. The owner is wearing a red masquerade type mask and black knee pads. He offers me a joint and says, "Looks like you got punched." I smoke it and hand it back to him with a blood spot on the spleef. He doesn't notice. As I set up, the headache starts and I'm convinced I have a blood clot or an aneurism and I'm going to have a seizure and die during this orgy shoot. One of the ladies they've hired is so fucked up that she's tangled in her heels and big white panties, rolling backward off the mattress. The pictures I get are gross and tragic and nauseating and my head and gums are throbbing. And I've got to get out of here.

"Where ya goin'?" asks the masked man.

"I'm going home."

"Home?"

"I have a . . . thing. I forgot about this thing."

"You just got here."

"I'll send you the good ones."

"You work for Leo, right?"

"No. We work together."

"Tell him to call me," he says, and takes one of the women by her ponytail. "Did you hear me, kid?"

Dear David,

I agree. The raspberries paths are the best part of the compound. And no, you never told me you used to hide there during minyon and Shabbos services. I'm sorry it's taken so long to write back. I'm sorry the pictures you sent me were returned. All the mail here goes into one bin in the office and it's sorted by a seventy-five-year-old rabbitzin. I think she sends back the letters from boys or goyim, especially boys who are goyim. It makes me so mad. Which pictures did you send me? I'm so sad I can't see them. It's raining hard here today but it didn't start until noon. In the morning my group beat group Shin in a tug of war and steal the hamantashen, which is exactly like steal the bacon without the traif. The win means we get a second helping of dessert for Shabbos tonight. Vanilla marble swirl. Shabbos here is easier than other days and makes everyone in a good mood. We use the outdoor sanctuary, which is just behind the new synogogue, to the right of the baseball field and the creek. Remember that? The rabbi allows us to wear white tops now and the sight of the clean white blouses look beautiful against the purple sunset. From the women's section I can look through a small hole in the *mechitzah* and see the men dancing. The amount of them is remarkable, so many more than last year. The floor becomes a black lake of men and it moves and ripples and hops, all in the name of Hashem. It's pretty powerful. I will write again as soon as I can. I'm very sorry the pictures came back to you. If you send them again, don't put a return address on it. I love you and hope you're not mad.

D.

The black and whites I sent all came back from Maine. The envelope had been opened and placed in a larger folder. The first one is of Debra at the compound, three years ago, picking raspberries with some girl. The rest are on the beach in Atlantic City. She runs from me, laughing, kicking sand. And Sarah. Barefoot, in a dress down to her ankles, her mouth wide, her arms like wings. A girl like that. With her clothes off. I'm sad for her. I pray she's okay. I pray in my own way. I hear my father and Brandi at the door. I'm not in the mood to explain so I shut my eyes.

"Hello!" he says, and I turn on my side. "David?"

"You're yelling in my ear, Martin."

"He had three jobs today."

"Isn't that his bag?"

"David?" he yells. "You here?"

"Stop barking, Martin."

I'm asleep, I say to myself. *I didn't hear you come in, must have been dozing.*

"So tell me all about her," Brandi says. "I hear she's a real dynamo in the sheets."

"You think you're funny, don't you?"

"Cobwebs in the pooter. That should be her stage name."

"Real sweet, Arlene. You have such a way with words."

"I know you slept with her."

"That's a flat-out lie. If you don't know the facts, then why speak at all."

"Is that what you used to tell Mickey?"

"And keep her the hell out of this."

"When you used to meet me at the Holiday Inn. I can hear it now, 'If you don't know the facts, Mickey, then why speak at all.'"

"You're exhausting, Arlene. I don't have to answer you."

"No, you don't. Because you have no soul, Marty. You just want to keep me around so you don't look so old and alone."

"I want to be alone."

"Then go already!"

"You're in my apartment. Right? You're all over me. Go get a life of your own already. Who needs you?"

There's a precious moment of silence. I wrap my pillow around my head. It's like being back in New Jersey with my parents. The sport of spitting on each other.

"Stop being a horse's ass and maybe I'll keep you around."

"Did I stand by you? Did I?"

"And I thanked you."

"Chemo?"

"And I thanked you."

"All those weeks."

"Thank you."

"You're not welcome."

"Sorry to hear that."

"Who are you close with? No one. I wonder why?"

"I'm close with lots of people, Arlene. The more they stay out of my life the more I like them."

"Like Debra?"

Silence.

"I'm *here*," I yell into my pillow, and my mouth stings.

"You let her get away, just like you're doing with me."

"She's better off without me."

"Maybe I am too."

"Then go already."

"I will. You watch."

"I'm watching. Go."

"You let a lunatic steal your daughter."

Pause.

"That's your only goddamn weapon? Debra? And this makes you worthy of what? Living with me? Why don't you and Ira open up your own whorehouse and leave me the hell alone."

I jump out of bed and throw my door open. "I'm *heeeere*!"

"David?" my father says. "What are you doing?"

"I'm sleeping!"

"Oh. Sorry. We just got home."

"Really?"

Brandi walks out of the kitchen like a punished child.

I close my door.

The sporadic sleep I get takes me into the night, through the smell of dinner, all the way to my father's steady snoring. The clock reads midnight, then 2:16 a.m.. At 6 a.m. I'm wide awake and my lip is so bubbled and tight that it might pop and spray the mirror with pus and goo. I go back to bed and see Sarah in a dream. She's on the beach in her Hasid clothes, kicking sand. We are alone and she kisses me. Until Leo arrives. He's wearing a sombrero, which Sarah pulls off his head. She's got it on.

"Going in early," my father says, rubbing my back. "Meeting with Ira. What time you coming in?"

"Still sleeping."

"What?"

"Dreaming."

"I need you today. It might get messy."

Your Child

ON THE CORNER OF BROADWAY and Eighth a woman is holding up a poster on a stick. The picture is of a naked woman being crammed into a meat grinder.

"This is your *child*. Reduced to chopped meat by *smut peddlers* and *pimps*. What happened to the little girl you brought to this earth? How did you let her become *this*? Help her. Pull her from the jaws of this machine."

She camps out here every Thursday morning, about fifteen feet from our front door. When she sees me today, she holds her sign high above her head and walks at my pace, her shoulder pinned to mine, her determination heightened. "This is *your* child!"

"I hear you," I always say, but she never hears me. I see Jocko out front with his ladder and box of marquee letters.

"Give the kid a break," Jocko says to her. "Buzz the hell off!"

"This is someone's child—"

"We know," he says.

"*Your* child," she says.

"I don't have a child, lady," he says.

She stares at me before sneezing, and slowly heads back to her corner.

"My dad here?"

"What the hell happened to your face?" he says.

"It's . . . I don't want to . . . Where is he?"

"Inside with Brandi and Ira. They're all bitchin' about something. You want some ice?"

"What are you putting up?"

He bends to lift a G from the bucket of letters and looks up at the marquee. "Gang bang," he says. "I think Ira's pushin' too fast. You watch, your dad's gonna be pissed at me. He likes to have a heads-up, right? I mean who doesn't? A gang bang? At the Imperial?"

"THIS IS YOUR CHILD." Through a bullhorn now. "REDUCED TO CHOPPED MEAT BY SMUT PEDDLERS AND PIMPS."

"Ira booked a gang bang?"

"Next week. I mean he's got real balls, that's all I'm gonna say. Anything for a buck, right?" He reaches in his pocket for a flask and tips it to his lips.

"Where's Leo?"

"Oh, he found a telephone booth for sale on Mott Street. You'd think he found the Holy Grail. Says he needs help getting it off the van in Brooklyn. He was looking for you."

"A phone booth?"

"Yup."

"For a porn flick?"

"He's really excited."

Last year Leo decided to make his first porn film. Tiki and a guy named Stew having sex on an empty N train. It became something of a local hit at the Imperial. He's made twelve or so more in recent months and now wears a beret when he shoots and yells "Action!" at the top of his lungs.

"He can't just use a mattress?"

"David?" says a soft voice behind me. She's wearing large, white sunglasses and a brown suede skirt. It's relief I feel most—to see her face, to see her dressed. I smile and my bruised skin stretches and aches.

"I'm really happy you're here," I say.

She reaches to touch my face, her eyes focusing on my mouth.

"Jocko, this is Sarah."

He offers his hand.

"REDUCED TO CHOPPED MEAT BY SMUT PEDDLERS AND PIMPS."

"He hit you," she says.

"No, no."

"You David's girlfriend?" Jocko says.

She smiles at me. "No."

"Cuz he really needs one. We all tell him."

"Let's take a walk," I say.

Jocko pats me on the back with his tongue out and Sarah and I cross the street. “I heard you at the door,” she says. “I saw him hit you. I came out right after but you were gone.”

“We don’t have to talk about that.”

“I know. You must have a lot of questions.”

“You left your family?”

She nods. “My mother talks to me. Listen, it’s a long, fucked-up story.”

We look at each other and she’s embarrassed.

“It’s not safe, Sarah.”

“I’ve never felt unsafe.”

“I don’t believe you.”

“I haven’t.”

“Maybe you should try typing,” I say, and her lips harden, a little shocked. “Or how about—?”

“It’s good enough for you.”

“I never said that.”

“I don’t need your advice or your opinion of me, David. I live alone now. Okay? All I do is stand there, nothing else . . . and they pay me.”

“Just stand there?”

“Stand there.”

“Nude.”

“Big deal. It’s not like I’m—”

“It’s a long way from yeshiva.”

“I didn’t come here for a lecture.”

“Okay.”

“I came here to tell you about your sister.”

Our eyes meet and she starts to smile.

"Where is she?"

"How long has it been since you've seen her?"

"Too long. Where is she?"

Over Sarah's shoulder I see Tiki's head pop out of the theater entrance. She's looking for someone.

"Brooklyn," says Sarah.

Holy mother of things large and small. There is no sound as my mind absorbs these words. Under my nose—all this time.

"I wasn't sure if I should tell you."

"She called you?"

"Yes."

"When?"

"Last week. She's getting married."

Thump, thump, thump, goes the heartbeat in my lip. Married. Right, good, seventeen years old. Perfect. Hasn't been permitted to be alone with a boy in her whole life. Of course married, wonderful, *mazel tov,* a wedding to someone bearded and smelly, like the butcher in *Fiddler on the Roof.* A singing man with a bloody apron and Theodore Bickel's face. *Od Yishama B'arai Yehuda U'vchutzos.* Let it speedily be heard in the cities of Judah and in the streets of Jerusalem, the sound of joy and the sound of happiness, the sound of my sister being forced to screw through a penis-sized hole in a sheet.

"You're upset."

"I need to see her," I say.

"She's in Kingsford, at her stepfather's apartment. Avram."

"Do you have an address?"

"David!" Tiki yells, finally spotting me. "Thank God. Come here, *quick*. It's your dad."

"What happened?"

"I don't know."

I run across the street and inside, where Brandi's in the lobby, teary eyed and shaken.

"Is he okay?"

"He just slapped Ira in the face. *Help* me."

"Slapped him?"

"Ira came into the office and started screaming. The next thing I see is your father's hand against his face. He's lost it this time."

"Where is he now?"

"He's up there," she says, pointing at the ceiling.

I bolt past the bar and the stage where an afternoon bachelor party is under way. My father and Ira are coming down the stairs.

"Dad!"

He faces me with fury in his eyes. "David, Get this fuckin' ass wipe away from me before I rip his throat out!"

"Hold on," I say. "Talk to me."

Ira's left eye is bruised. "I'm calling the cops," he growls.

"This motherfucker booked a gang bang. Ira booked a gang bang in *my* theater."

"It's a business move!" Ira says. "And it's my goddamn theater too."

"Just like the movies, Ira? Is that a business move too, or do you just want to see my wife getting *shtupped* on a cherry picker? Huh? Which is it?"

"That was *her* decision, Arbus! She's a grown woman. And she's not your wife until you marry her!"

"Where the hell are the fuck films of *your* wife, Ira, gettin' banged like a rag doll? I want to see those, I'll buy all of 'em without telling you so we can run 'em on every screen we got. Sound good, ya schmuck?"

"You act like *I* fucked her. They're old movies, Marty. It was *her* idea, anyways! How many goddamn times do I have to say it?"

My father walks right up to him again, his right fist clenched. Then Brandi appears and gets between them. "No more fighting!"

"C'mon, Dad," I say, but when I touch his shoulder he jolts away, glaring at Ira.

"Did you just say *you* fucked her?" he says.

"*No*, Martin, listen for a change. I said you're *acting* like I fucked her."

"Did you?"

"Of course not!"

"Did you?"

"I hate you, Marty," Brandi says. "I've had enough."

My father looks at me. "He just went and bought the films. Is that a scumbag or is that a scumbag? What else don't I know about these two?"

"I gave Ira permission," Brandi says.

"And why didn't you ask *me,* Arlene? Why ask this putz?"

"They're *classics*!" Ira screams. "It's a business move. It was twenty years ago for Christ's sake!"

"You're both lying to my face."

"Forget it," Ira says, "Just keep booking burlesque acts, Marty. I'm finished!"

My father's arms raise and he brings his fist down on his own leg. "Tell me right now if you fucked my girlfriend, Ira."

Ira waves his hand at him in disgust. "Go kill yourself, Martin. I'm tired of your bullshit! I'm a married man who's trying to make a buck for his family so go back to 1940 with your dear old dad and book all the crap acts you can find."

It's a knee-jerk thing, the leaping across Brandi and smashing Ira's face with his elbow.

"*Auuugh!*" Ira screams, holding his nose as his knees buckle.

"Jesus Christ," says Brandi, taking off her heels before kneeling to Ira. My father glares at the two of them before running away.

"Dad!" I'm chasing after him now. Sarah's with Jocko when I get downstairs. We all watch my father climb up on the stage. Tiki's got a bachelor on her lap, who's wearing nothing but his striped boxer briefs. "Jocko, call Leo," I yell.

"He's picking up the phone booth, remember? Why's your dad on stage?"

"Cut it off, cut the music off!" my father screams, waving

up at the sound booth. The music lowers and eventually stops. "Get off," he orders Tiki and the bachelor. "We're closing early. Get the fuck off my stage!"

Tiki runs off but the drunken bachelor puts his arm around my father. My dad shoves the guy away and he comes back for more.

"Get the hell away from me," my father barks.

"What are you doing to my party?"

"Look at you, you stupid pig. Pigs!" he says. "Look at all the pigs. Go home to your ugly mothers you pigs! Look at you. *You, you . . . you, you.* You'd all fuck *mud*! Horny scumbags!"

Brandi walks on stage and whispers something into my father's ear.

"Show us your cans!"

"Without further ado," Sal announces through the speakers, "over a hundred films and over a million rock hard fans and appearing in booths in constant loop downstairs in booths three, eight, and twelve, let's have a warm Imperial welcome for Las Vegas's own Ms. Veronica Saint *Jaaaames*!"

Veronica walks out, frightened, her eyes wide. She drops to her knees, bowing to my father, and Brandi leads him off the stage.

"What is wrong with you?" Brandi chastises him, but he's gone again, up the stairs.

"Let him cool off," she tells me. I follow him up there anyway, though, and watch him enter the empty peep chamber. I try to open the employee door in the back. It's locked so I go around and into one of the peep booths. It smells like B.O. and cleanser but the floor is dry. A miracle. As I put a token in the slot, the shade slowly lifts and there he is with his head in his hands, sitting on the pink circular mattress in the center of the room. He doesn't look up when I knock on the Plexiglas.

"Dad?" When he finally sees me I try to smile. "Unlock the door."

"No."

"Please."

"No!"

The hair on his head is pure white and matted to his scalp. He rubs his temples with fingertips, shakes his head. "I'm done," he says. "I did it and now I'm done."

It's silent as we both hear the bassy thump from downstairs. The sound of applause and whistles for Veronica.

"Will you let me in?" I say.

"Where were you?" he says, looking up at me through the Plexi. He can't see me. "I was outside."

"Doing what?"

"Talking to someone."

"Well I needed you."

"I have news, Dad."

"And I couldn't find you. When I need you I want you here. How am I supposed to find you if I need you?"

"I didn't know you needed me."

He nods, concedes, and we're silent for a while.

"Debra's back."

The shade starts to drop and I root around for more tokens. I only have one and I put it in the slot. There's my father, staring at me as the shade rises.

"She called?" he says.

"No. Sarah is downstairs. Remember Sarah?"

"No."

"Atlantic City. The rabbi's daughter. She knows where Debra is."

He lowers his head into his hands.

"Let's go together," I say. "We'll ring the doorbell."

"You still don't get it. I love her, she's my daughter, but she's been taught to hate me. Don't you get it?"

"She's getting married."

"Married?"

"I know." The shade drops again. "I'm out of tokens."

"She's sixteen years old."

"Seventeen, Dad. Her birthday was—"

There's a knock on the employee door. Then another. "Open the door," Brandi says. "Marty! Open this door."

"Talk to her," I say through the shade. "Just talk to her, Dad."

I don't hear anything and then he coughs. Brandi knocks again and I lean against the wall of the booth, just waiting for him to come out. The audience below us is loud for a minute and when it fades we're left with the music: "Lay down and boogie and play that funky music till you die."

"Is she gone?" he asks.

"Go talk to her."

"You love me," I hear my father say. "That's why you're in there. Because you love me."

My old man. He never says things like this. "I do."

"I deserved to lose her, ya know. We were both selfish parents."

"You didn't lose anything. She's in New York. Can we talk outside? So I can see you."

I hear him rise from the mattress and follow the sound of his footsteps. I meet him at the employee door. We pass the office and the dressing rooms without either of us being seen, then head down the stairs and through the theater, where the stage is empty but the bachelor party is in full swing. When we get to the lobby, Brandi and Ira are there. No Sarah.

"Did you see a girl?" I say.

"Instead of my calling the cops," says Ira, "Why don't you just pay for my X-rays out of pocket. I take cash."

"You're fine," my father grumbles.

"I'm not here for your morality, you cocksucker. I'm here because this is my business. Gang bangs make money all over the place, not just on the strip. Okay? Burlesque? Comedy? Willy Fuckin' Sapley? Are you kidding me? They don't bring in shit and never will again. I don't commute from Long Island every goddamn day to make friends. I'm here to pay my bills, Martin. Go live in West Palm Beach if it's too hot for you, pal. Because it's only gonna get hotter from here on in."

My father says nothing, just looks up at Brandi.

"Accusing me of adultery when I have a wife and children is pretty fucked up, Martin. You think after all these years I could think of such a thing." He laughs and looks up at Brandi, a full foot taller than him. "Okay . . . I'm not saying I haven't thought about it."

Brandi rolls her eyes and my father clenches his jaw, his teeth. He tries to calm himself by walking to the front window.

"I'm kidding, I'm kidding."

"He's kidding, Dad," I say, suddenly glimpsing Sarah outside. "Look. That's her. From Atlantic City, remember?"

My father lifts a sample dildo off the counter called Big Black John. He raises it like a machete above his head. "I'm just kidding too!"

"Wait, wait," I say, as my father swings it at Ira's face.

"Marty, stop!" Brandi yells, but he chases Ira. It's like two kids playing tag.

"Come here," my father barks. "Let me kill you with this thing!"

"You can't take a goddamn joke?" Ira says, but my father goes right after him.

"Dad, calm down. *Hey!*"

He swings Big Black John, gets a piece of Ira's shoulder. "Get this prick away from me, David!"

I watch my dad sort of skip closer and when he's in range he simply attacks the top of Ira's head with the weapon, relentless in his determination to hurt him. Two thwacks, three thwacks, four hard thwacks, until I grab his arm. Brandi hurls herself on top of him, her long body sprawled over him like a blanket. I pull Big Black John from his hand. Ira, the victim—his palm on his bald spot, his eyes still closed.

"That's it. I'm calling my lawyer!" he says, jumping up and running.

"I hate you, Marty," Brandi says, with a wobble in her voice.

"Yeah . . . well . . . *good*. If I ever hear you fucked that Jew bagel, I'm gonna hang myself. Go show your old fuck films, Arlene. Let the whole world beat off to movies you made at the turn of the century."

"You can't just talk to each other, can you?" I say. "It has to be a bite? Don't you hear how fucking tiring it is?"

"Look at him, David, he doesn't love me. He doesn't love anyone," Brandi says.

The door opens and a group of Jersey jocks come in. They lift up everything in sight, laughing. One of them finds a magazine called *Boobs and Bush*. He holds it up to his friends, who all roar, bending at the knees. "I'm buying this, I'm buying this, how much is it?" he asks me. I point to Brandi. "You work here, lady?"

"We're closed," she says, walking behind the counter.

"Forget the magazine, how much are *you*?" a different guy asks to her. "How much do you cost?"

"She said we're closed," my father says.

"Five bucks for the magazine," she says.

"But I said how much are *you*?"

"Enough," I tell him. "Just buy it and get out."

The guy steps up to me, chin to chin, and turns his baseball hat backward. "What'd you say?"

His friends gather around me and my father picks up Big Black John. "Who wants to fuck with me?"

"Dad."

"How much for a hand job?" someone says, and takes his wallet out.

Brandi eyes my father with great tedium in her eyes. "How much ya got?"

"Very funny, Arlene."

The kid reveals a wad of bills just as Leo walks in. He's carrying a tall houseplant that's blocking his face. "Girl out here wants to talk to you, David. She's *foxyyyyy*."

My father and Brandi both swivel to see who it is.

"I need you today," Leo says to me, putting down the plant. "I found a phone booth and I gotta get it to Kingsford. You seen Tiki?"

"It's Sarah," Brandi says, and points out at the street. "Look, David."

"I got fifty bucks," the Jersey jock says, plopping the money on the counter. Leo lifts the cash. Just as Sarah smiles and enters the store.

Sheitelmacher

What she'd see, if she saw us, from the window in Brooklyn: a white, dented van with a black man, an old man, and an ex-Hasid in the front seat with Leo's plant between her legs. Brandi and I split the back and behind us, where two rows of seats once were, the phone booth slides from side to side making a grating sound of weighty glass on steel.

Brandi touches my lip without asking me and I flinch from the pain.

"What the hell happened?"

"I don't want to talk about it."

Leo turns his head to me every time he hears the scraping noise. "Don't let it crack."

"It's bumping the spare tire thing," I say.

"Put your hand on it."

"I'd have to go back there."

"How much is that thing costing me?" my father says.

"Got it dirt cheap," Leo says.

"And what if someone cuts themselves on whatever's making that noise back there?"

"Nobody's going to get cut, boss."

"I bought three mattresses in May and you don't even use 'em."

"I use them all the time, Marty. It's boring already."

"What the hell difference does it make where they *shtup*? Just put 'em on the floor and push the button, Leo. This ain't *Ben Hur.*"

Sarah's the only one who laughs. My father's feeling better. "There," he says, pointing. "The Kingsford Bridge. The bridge that will drop me on my ex-wife's doorstep. She's going to be so happy to see me."

Sarah's got a nice laugh. What an audience for the old guy.

"She'll probably have a heart attack!" he says. "I'm not ringing the doorbell, I can tell you that."

"Big surprise," Brandi says. "Our fearless leader."

"What does that mean?"

"It means it's way, way past time someone steps up to that lady's door and says, 'Wake the hell up. You can't steal someone's kid.' Debra should choose the way she wants to live. Look at Sarah. I knew the second I met you, you were gonna run someday. Why? Because you're a fighter like me and you knew your life was going to suffer. Your parents and their selfish needs and fears and all that bullshit. Insecurities, disenchantment . . . fuckin' so stupid. My mother did it with food and booze. Mickey does it with *God*. With God! I don't know which is worse."

The van jolts forward and the phone booth shifts, bashing into the rear doors. "David. Please," Leo begs. "It's gonna end up on the road."

I make my way over Brandi's knees. She's got her fist against her chin and her eyes pinned on the bridge.

"You didn't put any blankets down, Leo."

"They're in Jocko's truck."

"Where are you bringing this thing?"

"I told you. It's goin' in the garden behind that loft in Kingsford. Where I shot *Three-Way Fuck Fest*."

I remember it well. Tiki on her back in a blue and yellow cheerleader uniform with Stewy Haynes on top of her, doing what Stewy Haynes does for a living. It reminded me of Wild Kingdom. Tiki, the antelope, and Stewy, with his teeth in her neck, waiting for her to stop quivering. His football pants were around his knees and his helmet strewn on a corner of picnic blanket. I knew then I could never do it. I'd never be the director on one of these shoots. There was such imbalance in the dance of it. Nothing sensual. Nothing poetic. Just nothing. The camera rolled all day, hooked on a tripod and Leo was pacing back and forth, occasionally coaching his actors on their objectives: to fuck each other.

I brace the phone booth with both hands but it still wants to slide so I sit on it and push against the back. No one is talking. My father grips the bottom of his seat with both hands. It's this van, the height and bounce of the chairs, but he looks so small, so vulnerable to me.

"Is it an apartment or a house?" he asks Sarah.

"I'm not sure," she says.

"But you know where it is."

"Yes."

"She told you?"

"I asked her."

"And who did she say she was marrying? Is he a rabbi or something?"

"His name is Micha and he's a purebred Lichtiger, not a *baal teshuva*. The fact that he asked her is very unusual; I mean a very big deal. It's unheard of, actually, a purebred and a *BT* writing in to the grand rabbi. When I spoke to her, though, she sounded unhappy about it. Or maybe just uncertain."

"Ohhhhhhhh boy, this is gonna suck!" My father pulls a cigarette from Leo's pack.

Brandi sits forward in her seat. "That's right, cancer-boy, light it up hot and juicy."

He ignores her and flicks the match out the window. "A goddamn sabotage is what it's gonna be. A ding-dong and a hello to you, Mickey, and she'll look at me like I have a swastika on each eyelid and I'll say, hey, that's my daughter over there and I am her father, I am her father."

"Maybe Sarah should ring the bell," I suggest. "See if they're even home."

Brandi nods. "I like that."

"I know," my father says, "I'll ring the bell and tell them I'm a plumber. 'Where's the fuckin' leak?' I'll say, and then we'll all rush the door and throw Debra in the phone booth. Mission accomplished. Or how about a battering ram?"

"Very funny," says Brandi.

"I can tell ya, back in the day, when I first met Mickey, I thought she was the sexiest thing I'd ever seen."

"Real nice," Brandi says. "Just great."

"The way she moved and her skin and her mouth. I couldn't keep my hands off her. But I'll tell you, she had some shitty parents. Too much inside her that couldn't be healed but everything," he says, now addressing me, "every little thing your mother said about me . . . was true. I *am* that person. If I were smart, I'd let them be. Just let them live their lives. I would not handle it this way."

"I'm sure you wouldn't. That's why she's been gone for two years, Martin. You didn't handle it *any* way."

"She *took* her, Arlene! She disappeared! To fuckin' Maine or Brooklyn or goddamn Tel Aviv!"

"You could've hired someone," Brandi says, "one of those cops who find people."

"Why the hell are you even in this car?"

"Great. Let me out. Leo, let me out!"

"Don't get out here," Sarah says. "It's just five more blocks up this way. You want to turn right here."

The pain in my stomach is fear.

"Stop here," Sarah announces. "It's there, it's that one I think: 6778. That gray building."

The apartment is blocked by an enormous tree. Both the middle and top front windows are hidden behind the trunk and branches. I lift my camera but even with my zoom lens, I can't come close to seeing inside.

"Holy shit," my father says. "My little girl is up there." He stands from his seat and moves next to Brandi in the back. He takes her hand in his and kisses it. "She's right up there," he says.

"Now you love me again."

"I'll go," I say.

"Or I'll go," says Sarah. "I'll just say I was in the neighborhood and see if Dena will come outside."

"I love you," I say, and everyone turns. "I mean for volunteering."

"David's got a *girl*friend?" Leo says, now out of the van, making his way back to his phone booth.

"If she comes out of there," my father says, "I may just collapse."

"Tell her you're sorry instead," Brandi says. "Just keep saying sorry, I'm sorry I was a jerk and I'll spend the rest of my life making it up to you. Something like that."

She kisses the tip of his nose as he swipes at his eyes.

"They're home," I say, zooming in on Sarah leaning into the intercom, speaking to someone. Now she's running back, across the street to the van.

"She's at the *sheitelmacher*'s," she says. "It's two blocks from here."

"Who did you talk to?" I ask.

"Some old lady."

"What the hell's a shatelmaker?" Leo says.

"The wig maker. She's getting fitted for the wedding."

"Already?" my father says. "When the hell is it, tomorrow?"

"Two weeks," Sarah says.

"Okay," says Leo. "The place I'm shooting is four blocks from here. Let's get the booth off and we can keep looking for her if you want."

"Fuck that," my father says. "We came this far, let's go now. Did she tell you where the wig lady lives?"

Sarah nods. "I know where Miri lives." She points behind us and Leo gets back in the driver's seat. Three minutes later we're in front of a beige Victorian house with a brick driveway and a sign on the lawn. GOD DOES NOT WATCH OVER THOSE WHO DO NOT OBSERVE TORAH.

"This is gonna work," my dad says. "Go tell your sister that her father's outside, waiting for her."

"I'm not going in there."

"Why the hell not? You're owed."

"What if mom's in there?"

"Even better. We've got momentum on our side. Go. Don't think about it, just go."

Sarah and I walk up the driveway together. She points to the door that leads to the basement. It has a bell on it and a sign that reads MIRI's in elaborate script. Through the window in the door I can see a row of lit vanity bulbs on the far side of the room. Ten or twelve walls of high shelving are arranged in the center of the space. I try the doorknob and it's open so I push it a bit and peek in. "It's open," I say.

"David," she says.

"It's open."

"I had two fittings here before I left. Miri does not like me." She leans forward and her mouth is against mine. "Good luck," she says, and leaves me.

"Sarah . . . *Sarah!*"

It takes a few minutes of standing, still tasting the kiss from the Hasid who ran off. But finally I open the door. I hear and see no one. The shelves are army green and metal and it's more like thirty of them. I step in and I'm between rows of shelves on which sit many small shoe box-sized containers. Each box has a sticker on it. The ones closest to me say CAUCASIAN EUROPEAN, HANA'S OWN, THE ALLY, THE ELEVEN-FIFTY. As I move further down the aisle, toward the vanity bulbs, I hear a woman's voice.

"Hello?" I say, way too quietly. The farther I walk down the aisle, the more I hear that woman's voice.

"Not fifteen!" she says. "Five oh."

I stop and squat, the lights about ten feet away.

"Fifty percent European human and fifty percent Koneculon. *Rifkah!*" the voice screams and two shelves away from me a head pops up. It's a young woman with a sheet-white face and a black wig.

"Yes, Miri."

"Get me four multilong, custom brunette Europeans and a half dozen of the half-n-halfs."

"Dark brown?"

"And a custom one fifty-two and a Jolie with cinnamon highlights."

"Yes, Miri."

The girl disappears into the stacks of shelves to my left. I stay frozen, listening to the sound of containers being opened. The bell on the door jingles behind me so I run to the aisle to my right. It's my mother. She's so small. She has a cup of coffee in her hand. I don't remember her ever drinking coffee. She walks toward the woman's voice and I listen to her steps, watching her through the gaps in the shelving.

"*Shalom aleichem*, Miri."

"Look at your *sheitel*, Miriam, it's, it's . . ."

"What?" my mother says.

"Have you been washing it?"

"Of course."

"Only cool water?"

"Yes, yes."

"How often?"

"What's wrong?"

"Looks thirsty," Miri says. There's a sneeze and then another, my sister. I hear her voice in it.

My mother laughs lightly. "Today, let's think about Dena."

"I understand, but please, do *not* use a standard hairbrush on it."

"I don't, Miri. I use the one you gave me."

"Because here, feel it, touch right here. Tension on the

follicles will stretch them. But, okay, you're right, enough about you. Now, Dena, you'll need six *sheitels* total."

And now I see Debra. She's sitting on a chair, like one in a beauty parlor.

"With the family you're marrying into, it would be *ash-unda, poot, poot,* to use synthetics. The father is from the grand rabbi's home, yes?"

"Yes," my mother says.

"Mazel tov."

"Toda Raba."

"Six wigs?" my sister says. I stand from my crouch and from here I can see her chair in the reflection of the mirror.

"Two for everyday life, two for Shabbos and . . . look at all this hair. This will need to be thinned."

"I'm not cutting today," my sister says. "I'm just matching color today."

"I won't be able to fit anything on," says Miri.

"I don't want it cut."

"I didn't say *cut,* I said *thinned.* Your wedding is when?"

"Two weeks," my mother says. "August seventh."

"Which synagogue?"

"Beth Tikvah."

"We must do a fitting today or it won't be ready. If it fits badly at your *Sheva Bruchas* the women will be laughing at *you.* Now! I match and design for brunettes better than anyone in the world. Are you listening?"

"Yes."

"Synthetics, even if treated perfectly, will begin to show signs of wear in six months."

"I think we're out of the Jolies," says Rifkah as she joins them. "But here is an Indonesian brunette."

"Oh, this will be perfect for the wedding. This is pure human hair. What do you think?"

"Lovely," says my mother. "What do you think, Dena? Isn't it beautiful?"

"It's . . . brown."

"It's the best hair in the universe," Miri says. "Look at it. Weight, *perfect,* strength, *perfect,* texture and high protein content, *perfect.* Okay, good, we like it, let's try it on. I'll snip one inch from the weight."

"No," my sister insists. "I just want to pick color today."

"*Two* weeks," Miri shouts. "Two weeks and you will become a woman in the eyes of Hashem! This is not a game, you're here now, I'm not a butcher."

"I don't want to cut it today."

"Then you're making my job impossible."

"Dena!" my mother says. "A little you could lose."

"I don't care." She is firm.

"Okay, first let's try it on without cutting. Maybe we'll have a miracle. Now, with this product you can place it on a wig stand and go from curly to straight with an electric curler or pin curlers. From twelve to fifteen wearings in spring and summer and six to eight wearings in fall and winter until washing it. Humidity and air quality are big factors so depending—"

"It hurts!" Debra says.

"Where?" Miri asks. "*Hey!* Until you buy it, let me do the touching, yes?"

"Take it off," Debra says. "Please, just get it off me."

Miri laughs. "It must be the wafting, your hair is too long."

"Please take it off."

"So touchy, this one. How about now? I moved it. Is it better?"

"A little."

"Scissors and comb. I'm only trimming the back where you're snagging. Nothing more. You are not a little girl anymore, yes? You need to act like the *kallah* you will become."

I hear a screech and brace myself to run. It's then I see my sister moving toward me so I turn and dart for the door. When I get outside I tear off around the building and down the driveway but I don't see the van. No van. I start to run but where, which way, so stupid that they'd do this. Harrison Street, Mailson Street, a village of stores and Hasids everywhere. No van, no white van anywhere. Where the fuck did they go? To unload the stupid phone booth? I get to a street called Blake and I'm pretty sure it links up with Morrison, the street my mother lives on. Five minutes later I see the apartment building. From the other side of the road, I look up at the tree, the windows beyond it. I make out a vase on the sill and the grand rabbi on the wall. Two men walk through the lobby and come out the front door. One of them stops when he sees me.

"Can I help you?" he says. As he looks at me, I watch his face grow confused beneath the brim of his hat. It's Avram. I remember him from Sarah's house, when her sister announced her marriage. Red bearded with circular frames.

He says something to his friend in Yiddish, then looks up at his window. My stepfather.

"It's me," I say, approaching him. "David."

"I know."

He nods and smiles through the strain on his face. "We met once."

"How are you?" I say.

"You look older," he says.

I can see his mind working, just wishing he'd stayed inside. His friend looks down, contemplating his shoes.

"We have *shul,*" Avram says.

"Can I talk to you?" I say. In his eyes I see the worry. When he removes his fedora there's a black velvet yarmulke underneath. He rests his hand on it and sighs. "You're not the only one," he says.

"What?"

"I mean, I know other families at the compound who have this problem. *Baalai teshuva* with family members who are not interested. So you're not the only one."

"Oh."

"I guess my first thought for you is whether you want to repair your relationship with your mother. I think you need to understand, deeply, who she is now. And what her life has become. I also would say she needs to understand who you are."

"You would? I mean, you do?"

"Of course. When it comes to Hashem, and the laws of *halakhah,* the lessons are complicated. It's never easy for young people, especially from split families like yours because . . . you have a father who doesn't believe in anything, really, so you haven't been given the chance to learn, to listen, to understand Torah or Talmud. In fact a child of a *baal teshuva* is—"

"Can I say something?"

He hadn't been looking at me but now he blinks a hundred times and our eyes meet.

"I'd like to give my sister some photographs. Pictures I took of us."

"Okay."

"I don't have them with me right now. But I can come back."

"I think I should warn your mother."

"Warn her?"

"Tell her. I'll tell her."

Avram looks to the sky before holding his index finger up to his friend. "Every Jew, David, no matter how his life has unfolded, has the opportunity to begin again." He reaches in his jacket and takes out a pen. "This is my phone at my office." He writes it on a piece of scrap paper from his pocket then hands it to me. "Think about your life and where you are. Think about your mother and sister. We choose to make sacrifices in the life we live, and we make them to respect ourselves and to respect Hashem, God. I think you should think about what it means to have your sister and mother in your life."

I see the van. Leo is driving two miles per hour past the apartment. I lift my arm and when he sees me he guns the engine before screeching to a stop.

"Get in!"

"What?" I say, looking behind me at Avram.

"Your dad."

I get in the van and Avram is still standing there. "I'll tell her I saw you," he says.

Leo floors the accelerator and I fall between the front two seats. "He had a thing, an attack. We called an ambulance from a house over there."

"An attack."

"He was holding his arm like this, gripping it and he was in pain, real bad pain."

"Go faster."

"I didn't know where a hospital was and neither did that girl."

He pulls to a stop across the street from the wig maker and points to a gray house. I run across the lawn and up the porch steps and into the front hallway and I see him there in the living room, unconscious, just lying on this stranger's plastic-covered sofa.

"Dad," I say, and my mind flashes to my sister's face. I hear a child crying, the sound of weeping, and Brandi is on her knees rocking back and forth, her hands pinned together. "I told him, I told him."

"Daddy?" I touch his earlobe for some reason, just stroke the shape of it, the softness. "Don't," I whisper, and Leo shouts, "David! They're here, they're here, get out of the way."

"They're here," I tell him. I hear a walkie-talkie hiss and a dispatcher voice.

"Where is he?" a paramedic says, pushing me out of the

way to attack my father with violent jerking motions that droop his head back.

"Don't hurt him," I say, knowing it sounds stupid.

"Is he alive?" Leo yells at them. My father's skin, his lips, his hands—all have a white dust on them.

"Don't die, Marty!" says Brandi and one of the men plunges a needle straight into my father's heart. He doesn't budge and one of them pounds his chest with his fist.

"Nothing," the paramedic says, and presses a stethoscope to his chest.

I reach out my arm and hold my father's hand. "It's fine," I tell him. Every word he ever said to me, every memory we shared is water now and leaking through the floorboards.

"Are you his son?" a man says behind me, and I see the family who lives here, standing by the staircase. Hasids. Six of them, five children and a man. A little girl sucks her thumb and stares at the person on her couch.

"Yes I am," I say, just as Sarah runs in the house, out of breath.

"He couldn't breathe, David. He asked for you. I told him you were close. That you'd be right back. Is he okay?" She gets on her toes to see him, to get a glimpse of his body on the couch.

"No," I tell her. "No. He's not."

Lieberman and Wise

I SEE HIM. IN THE shallow of a dream. But it isn't his hair or his voice or even his face anymore. It's someone else's father with his own son on the beach, and the sand is black. The boy is blocked from the sun by a white, flowing sheet and he's talking to the man, softly, before it all fades amid the sounds of the ocean, that gentle constant, the in and out of the waves.

"Hello? Who's there?" I say, sitting up in my father's bed. I don't remember choosing to sleep here.

"It's time," Brandi says from the hallway.

Time to bury my dad.

The gunshots are as steady as a metronome. The shooting range next door. Pop, pop, pop, pop, like the person pulling the trigger is learning to play "Chopsticks." From the gravesite, I watch Leo and Jocko and Tiki all flinching every time another round is fired. Sarah arrives with the rabbi she found, a guy with Art Garfunkel hair. He tells me I'm the only "official" mourner because Jewish law says you're not technically a mourner if you're not the father, mother, son, daughter, sister, brother, or spouse of the deceased.

"You'll speak after I say a few prayers," he says.

"I'd like to speak too," Brandi says.

"Are you a direct relative?" he asks.

"No," she says.

"Then, please, I only want the immediate family to participate. It's tradition."

She's not happy. Sarah whispers something into her ear but it doesn't help. We all walk up to the gravesite but Brandi stays back. I try to wave her over, but she's angry, her back to us now. Jocko goes back down to get her but she won't listen to him. I can't worry about her right now. The coffin is pine and unpainted and looks as cheap as it did in the funeral home. But apparently Jews believe that you leave the world in a simple box, wrapped in clothing with no pockets and a shroud of linen or muslin. He didn't believe in any of this but now, as he lies here in that box, there are still rules about who can talk and who can mourn. I'm so sorry for him. In there alone, a stranger's *tallis* around his shoulders. I'm sorry that the most religious day of his life is today.

"Oh, Lord, what is man that you should care about him, mortal man that you should think of him? Man is like a breath, his days are like a passing shadow. O Lord bend your sky and come down; touch the mountains and they will smoke . . ."

In the parking lot I see Ira with his wife and some other man. Brandi has no choice but to walk with them now.

"Rescue me, save me from the mighty waters, from the hands of foreigners, whose mouth speaks lies, and whose oaths are false."

I feel Leo's hand on my back and it triggers the loss, the weight of where I'm headed. I swallow again and again to avoid tears and the effort is tiring, nauseating. The rabbi says a bunch in Hebrew, then says my name. "You ready?" he says.

I step closer to the grave and look down into it. The walls have roots sticking out of the cracks in the mud. My grandfather's plot is three feet away.

"I was told I'm the only mourner here today," I say. "But we all know that's not true." A light drizzle starts and the rain begins to darken the pine. "His family was his father, Myron. His daughter, Debra. Me, David. And of course you, Brandi."

She takes the moment to smirk at the rabbi.

"I miss you already. I wish we could have said a few more things. I didn't know you were going . . . when you did. If you hear me, I want you to know I love you. And I'm going to miss you."

After a long silence, the rabbi signals the two cemetery workers, who lower the box into the ground. He asks me to lift the shovel and scoop some dirt on the coffin. A symbol, he tells us, of the finality of my father's life and the reality of death, according to Judaism, the religion into which he was born.

I do it, I get some on the tip of the shovel and toss it down onto the box. The dirt hits it with an empty sound and most of it slides off the sides. It is a raw and sobering ritual, assisting in the task of his burial. The rabbi takes the shovel, says another prayer in Hebrew but before he finishes, Brandi takes the shovel from his hands. Her scoop is much bigger and hits the box with a muddy plop. She hands it back to the rabbi. She's crying hard as she walks down the path and into the parking lot. Ira kisses me on the lips and I feel cold, man saliva on my mouth.

"Anything you need. Anything you want. The theater is half yours. Your father was family to me. We had our moments but he was a brother, my older brother. You saw us fight, I know. But you also saw us hug. Let's you and I hug now."

We do.

"So we're good? We can work together?" Ira says.

"I have to go now."

"What about your sister?"

Ira speaks louder because I'm moving away from him. "You're right. Let's do it at a more respectful time."

I head down the path to the beat of gunfire and decide I'll never see Ira Saltzman again.

"You should call her now," Sarah says. "She should know."

"Yeah? Well maybe she should call me."

"It's her father, David."

"I didn't want a Lichtiger funeral. I told you that."

"I could call her."

"I'll do it."

"Will you stop?"

Running, yes, from the grave, from Ira, from telling my sister. "I just want to go home, Sarah. Can I drive you somewhere?"

"Leo said he'd give me a ride home."

"Leo? He did?"

"Brandi should've been able to speak," Sarah says, trying to change the subject.

She's looking at me, wanting me to feel jealous and I do.

"I guess I'll see you later," she says, and climbs in the back of Leo's Dart. From my father's car I see her lighting a cigarette. She holds it high, between her middle and pointer fingers, like someone taught her how. A shotgun blast is heard and my shoulders flinch at the noise. Sarah looks at me as if the world just shook. And I drive home.

Oliver Twist

I FOUND SOME RUM. I like it with juice, this red juice I bought at a deli on the corner. I drink it until it gets dark and then I fall asleep on my dad's bed. When I wake up the "Star Spangled Banner" is playing in the living room. It's creepy somehow, in the blue light from the TV, a flag waving in slow motion. My scrotum stretches like Silly Putty so I wrap it around my finger like a dumpling and realize I'm drunk. I start to jerk off but feel like a scumbag, like one of the regulars at the Imperial with their pants at their ankles. I can't sleep. The phone rings at 4 a.m. but when you're dead you're not there to pick it up. Hello? Are you there? Is it you? No, I'm dead. I can't talk to you now. In fact I'll be dead for quite some time and will never be able to speak to you again. The most precise word in the English language. How long? Never. How about after that? After never? It rings again and it's stupid how I lift my head from the pillow to look at the receiver until it stops. Ring, ring, fucking, ring, ring all you want. What do you want anyway? Oh, you want to *talk* about my dad. You want to console me, to help me, to put your skin on mine for warmth because you know I am Oliver, the orphan boy. Ringing again, five thirty, it's the tax man, the police, the garage, Larry Abromowitz. It's his dry cleaner, his barber, some stripper he once knew. I throw one of Brandi's pink pillows at the phone and it spills onto the floor. "If you'd like to make a call, please hang up and try again." You sound nice, lady, you sound really swell. No more calls, please. I'm an orphan now and don't need to pick up the phone if I don't want to. The view from my dad's bed is the flat rooftop of a post office and I see puddles of rain and a yellow kickball floating in one of them. At six the neighbor upstairs is jumping in place or maybe it's jump rope, yeah, the tap, tap, tapping on the floor is the rope. If I try to keep up with him, I need to leap like a toad, like a pogo stick, straight up and down. As soon as I land I hop even higher and I've never been much of an athlete but I think if I try, *hup, hup, hup*, I could place my palms on . . . the . . . ceiling.

I hear a knock on the door and tiptoe to look through the peephole. It's Ira.

"You in there or what?"

I stay as quiet as a tree no one hears, a bird in the wind, a farting mouse. Knock, knock, knock. Go away Ira, go the hell away. Not here, out to lunch, visiting relatives on a patch of land in the Baltic Sea.

"I know you're in there, David. I can hear you."

I sit on the floor, one wall away.

"You're missing print jobs, kid. People are calling in for ya. If you don't want 'em I'll find someone who does."

Through the peephole his nose is huge. Moist little hairs rooted in the cavern of the round tip. He stands there for five minutes sighing and giving my eye the finger. Finally he leaves.

Three slices of American cheese, a jar of apricot jelly, blue-crusted Wonder bread and two double A batteries in the slot for eggs. What a feast. I eat in his bed and see his suit pants on the chair by the window, black and forgotten, like a pair of legs left behind. What now, say the pants, the belt drooping off the chair to the floor. Stuck there for eternity, a pair of paralyzed slacks, longing to get to the closet where their matching blazer resides. I try them on—they're a little short around the ankles but fine in the waist. The interior is silky and cool against my skin and I see no reason to wear anything else for the rest of my life. Doorbell. I freeze.

"David, it's Brandi. What are you some kind of hermit now? My key is still missing. I left some of my clothes in the closet." Doorbell. "David, I know you're in there. I can hear the television."

Her nose is narrow and powdered. There are no hairs for miles and miles. The wig is curly and tight and she pulls on the bangs.

"I could send a cop in," she says. "I might be saving your life."

....

Don't do that. Please don't do that. I wonder if she even has hair under that wig. Or actual skin beneath the goop she puts on. She rings the bell twice before leaving.

My father has shoe trees in his closet, an iron bowl of pennies, a tuxedo with dandruff on the shoulder, and a mountain of dry-cleaner plastic. There must be ten pairs of women's shoes and two dozen dresses. Wig boxes galore. I find another one of his suits. A white three-piece. It smells like cigarettes and cologne, a battle of nicotine and chemical musk. I decide to put it on. Debra used to get nauseous from the cigarette smell and she'd steal the packs from his jackets and stab them with a protractor. She hid them too, buried them in the yard in Newstead and in the gully behind the Slaters'. Dear Debra, Dad is . . . really sick. Dear Debra, Dad was sick and he died so now you know. Dear Debra, when is your wedding to the butcher in *Fiddler on the Roof*. I have some news. About Dad. Dear Debra, is your fiancé a bearded man in *tzitzit* who raises his arms when he dances in circles and snaps simultaneously with both hands saying, *oy, oy, oy,* will you marry me, Dena, *oy, oy, oy,* will you be the seventeen-year-old mother of my eleven children? Moses and Isaac and Ezra and Solomon and Tabernacle and Esau and Dear Dena. Dad is gone. *May my family ever be perfect in your sight*. Grant me light, lest I sleep the sleep of death.

I fall asleep on the couch still in his white suit. I'm dreaming of hundreds of Hasidim, an ocean of undulating hats and wigs. I'm not invited to the wedding but I stand under the *huppah* with my sister, the bride, and her husband, the butcher, and I walk around her seven times and my mother is stunned that I know this ritual and it makes her love me. I can see it, she loves me. She's proud of me, finally at peace with herself and her son. She grips the brim of my fedora and shakes it, smiling.

I wake up and stare at the phone still off the hook. I have to tell them. *Hup, hup, hup,* he died, *hup, hup, hup . . . hup . . . hup . . . hup.*

I hear a key, metal in metal, and the door is opening. "Hello!" I yell, and slowly poke my head out of my father's room. Brandi Lady.

"I knew it," she says.

"You knew what?"

"You didn't kill yourself," she says, pulling off her white opera gloves. "Ira thinks you killed yourself."

I sit on the couch, my back to her.

"It smells in here."

"No it doesn't."

"And the phone's off the hook. Leo's been calling you for days. And you've wrinkled the hell out of your father's suit. Have you been sleeping in it?"

I look down at the lapels, the crease in the pants. "Your clothes are in the closet."

"Why did you take the phone off the hook?"

"It was ringing."

"Why aren't you coming to the theater?"

"Because I quit." I look right at her.

She puts both hands on her cheeks and stares back at me. "Oh yeah?"

"Yeah."

"Okay, then. Maybe Sarah will take your place. She's been coming in every day since the funeral."

I watch her go into the kitchen.

"To the theater?"

"Yup," she says, and I hear her put the receiver back in its cradle.

"She's a Hasid, Brandi."

"She *was* a Hasid."

"Don't let her do it."

"Don't let her do what? She's her own person. Sorry," she says, "I'd be a hypocrite if I told her to leave."

"Then just be an adult."

"Ya know what? I'm not telling an eighteen-year-old girl what she can and can't do."

"Then get *out*! Get the fuck *out*!" I open the door for her but she doesn't budge.

"You sure are angry. Why don't you scream. Do it. *Screeeeam!*"

"Stop."

"You want to hit something, David? Do it, do it now, get it out, man!"

"I don't need you to root for me, *Ar*lene."

"Oh, be real," she says behind me. "You're hurting, look at you. I want to be here for you, I'm trying to be here for you."

Be real? Be real? What a joke. I have to laugh at this person in her opera gloves in July. "Be real?" I say. "Brandi Lady? No, sorry, Luna Von. I mean how many little dirty secrets do you have, Arlene Morrison, from some hick town in Michigan? I mean who are you, exactly? Do you even know? Which one of your characters is telling me to *be* fuckin' *real*?"

Her shoulders shrug. "Feel better?" she says.

"No! I've had enough bullshit."

"So I'm a phony?"

"Look at you, you look like a stripper. Who dresses like that in public?"

"I do, you jackass."

"Well why don't you be fuckin' real and buy a normal dress."

"Hey, hey, hey what's all the yelling about?" Leo is in the doorway. "I could hear the screaming all the way down the hall."

"You talk to him, Leo, he's being an asshole."

"Where the fuck is Sarah? Huh, Leo?"

He looks at Brandi first and then to me. "I haven't seen you in four days and that's all you got for me?"

"See what I mean?" Brandi says.

"Are you giving her work?"

"No. She's just been coming by the theater."

"For what?"

"I don't know. She asks if I've talked to you and I tell her your phone's off the hook."

"Is she there now?"

"No. I dropped her off at the set in Kingsford. She said she wanted to help out."

I run my fingers through my hair and give it a yank. "Help *out*? With what? Help out with what, Leo?"

"Listen, I came here to see if you were okay. Ira thinks you stuck your head in the stove. But I really don't like the way you're talking to me."

"Have you filmed her doing anything?"

Brandi and Leo exchange a look and Leo shrugs. "No."

"Good."

"But she's eighteen years old, ya know?"

It's the first time I've ever stepped up to him. The first time I've ever put my finger in his face. "Don't . . . touch . . . that . . . Hasid."

"I didn't."

I pull my father's jacket off and run down the hall to my own room to find the pants and white shirt I wore to the funeral. When I get back, Leo's whispering to Brandi and they both look pissed off.

"The loft, Leo. I want to *help* out too. Please. Take me to the loft."

BRANDI HAS TO come too. Just to nag me, I think. The whole ride to Brooklyn I listen to her talking about love and parenthood and child rearing and how so many people "fuck it up." Leo and I don't say a word but she doesn't care. She's in know-it-all mode and seems to have this particular speech prerecorded. Kids needs space and unconditional love, blah, blah, blah. When we arrive, I run from the van but find no one in the loft. There are dirty dishes in the kitchen and someone left the TV on.

"What a mess," Brandi says.

From the bathroom window, I can see Jocko and Tiki and that cock slinger Stewart Haynes.

"I don't see her," I say.

Brandi comes in and looks down at the garden. "What are they doing back there?" she says.

They're filling out college applications, they're painting a picket fence, they're practicing for a choir recital, they're helping a calf give birth, they're carrying an old, blind woman across the street, they're making a difference in so very many ways, utilizing their collective gifts to contribute to our precious planet.

"They're shooting a porno."

"Outside?" she says.

The garden is surrounded by tall fencing and even higher yellow shrubbery that blocks the view of any neighbors. The phone booth stands in the center of a patch of lawn. There are two cameras, one mounted inside the thing and the other outside the door. I don't see Sarah and am hoping she went home. I head down to the garden just as Tiki and Stewart get nude in the phone booth. Jocko is on his stomach on the grass, looking through the camera. "Hi, David."

"Hi. You seen that girl Sarah?"

He gets to his feet and looks around. "There she is."

She's filling a watering can from a garden hose. I tell myself to be calmer than I feel. She sees me before I get to her and turns off the water. "There you are," she says, eyes wide. "I was worried about you."

"What are you doing here?"

She looks down at the spigot. "I'm working."

"Working? Great. This is your *job,* now?"

"Why are you talking like that?"

"You shouldn't be here, Sarah."

"And why not?" she says, moving away from me.

I take her elbow in my hand and she yanks it away. "Please get off me."

"Come on, I'll take you home."

"No. I'm going to pour water over that phone booth. That's all I'm doing."

I step closer to her so I can whisper. "I don't want you working with Leo."

"*You* work with Leo."

"No, I don't. He just tells me who's hiring. I'm independent, remember?"

"What do you think I'm trying to be, David?" She takes the watering can and climbs the ladder next to the booth.

Leo comes out with a bagel in his mouth. "See, buddy. She's just helping out. Sarah? When I say action, just pour it over the phone booth, okay. Get it all wet. Tiki, Stewy, you ready?"

Tiki and Stewy put their cigarettes out and step barefoot

into the booth. "Good, just start kissing and go from there. Are we ready?"

"Ready," says Jocko.

"Okay, here we go. *Action!* Good. Let it rain, Sarah. Let it rain."

Brandi stands with me by the back door of the building. "You owe me a big apology," she says, but I ignore her.

Sarah tips the can and water beads down the glass as Tiki drops to her knees to pull the string on Stewart's sweatpants. It's revolting, watching a blow job next to my father's girlfriend so I walk away from her. No one speaks as the scene is shot but Leo paces back and forth. "Move her hair, Stewy," he says.

Stewart begins to moan as he puts Tiki's hair behind her ear.

"Your line," Leo says.

Stewart squints his eyes, trying to remember the script. "Line!"

"All I wanted was a dime," Leo says.

Stewart nods. "Alls I wanted was a dime."

Tiki smiles and looks up at him. "That's okay, you can keep the change."

Leo pumps his fist and looks back at us, smiling.

"Battery's dying, Leo." Jocko waves his arm. "Battery light."

"Cut!"

Tiki rises from her position with her hands on her hips. The rain stops. "What's wrong?"

"Where's the other camera?" Leo says.

Sarah steps down and heads back to the hose. "Can I talk to you alone?" I say in my kindest voice and no, I don't pull her, I never force her, but she's mad at me, fighting me. "No, you can't."

"I just want to talk."

"About what?"

"David," Brandi says. "Will you leave her alone?"

"She's leaving, it's fine."

"You're leaving, Sarah?" Leo says.

"Yes," I say. "We're going over to my sister's."

Sarah looks at me and puts the watering can on the ground. "Your sister's?"

"Yeah. I haven't told her yet."

"About your *dad*?" Sarah says. "You didn't tell her about your dad?"

"That's why I'm here. I'm going to head over there right now. I thought you'd come with me."

"Maybe you should go by yourself," she says.

They all stare at me and I see Jocko picking his nose.

"This is what you want, Sarah? To be one of these people for the rest of your life."

Stewart adjusts his dong in his sweatpants and steps up to me. "One of *these* people? What about you?"

"Exactly," Brandi says.

"He's having a bad day," Leo says. "A bad week. He doesn't mean it. Let's get back to it. Come on, where's the other camera?"

"That wig," I say to Brandi.

"Yeah? What about it?" she says.

"Nothing. Just that I lived with you for over two years and I've never seen your real hair. Maybe you're afraid. Afraid to be *real*."

"Oh boy," Leo says.

I step closer to her. "Do you even have hair underneath that thing? Or are you bald?"

Brandi and I stare at each other in silence and I watch her eyes fill with tears. The tip of her tongue is touching her top lip as she places her fingertips under the hairline and lifts the wig up and off her head. I can see her ears and her brown hair, short and cut very close to her scalp. "Happy now?" she says, throwing the wig in my face. When I bend to lift it she steps on it with her pointy heel. "Get out of here. Go. You don't want to be one of us? Then go."

"Come on, Sarah."

"Leave her the hell alone," she says. "There's nothing she needs from you. Go, David. Get out of here." She points to the back porch stairs. "We don't want *you* anymore."

Sarah is standing behind Leo, so I walk back into the apartment, through the hallway and toward the street. I have no memory of making the decision but I know what I have to do. I will go to my mother's home and tell her husband, Avram, what she used to be. A stripper. That's right. A better stripper than a mother. A better liar than a parent. I'm going to get a bullhorn and posters and tell everyone in the neighborhood what a phony fucking hypocrite Mickey Arbus really is. I'll hang flyers on all the telephone poles and call the grand rabbi himself. That's right, Rabbi, she's a *baal teshuva* who used to shake her tits in a dump called the Imperial Theatre.

"David," Sarah says.

She's in the doorway, a backpack over her shoulder.

"Are you going over there?"

I nod.

"I wasn't invited to the wedding," she says. "I don't think your mother likes me anymore." She comes down the steps and stands next to me in the middle of the road. "I'll go with you, David. But I'm not ringing the bell this time. And you have to be nice to me."

I offer her my hand. She looks at it before taking it and holding on tight.

Debra

THROUGH MY LENS I SEE the dark grooves of the tree trunk and the slow, tired movement of the summer leaves. We are across the street from their apartment building, along a fence, and the front door opens. I steel myself, ready to see my mother, but it's not her. A Hasidic woman with two small kids emerges. I see her through my camera—her eyes, her chin, the *sheitel* on her head.

"You ready?" Sarah asks.

"No."

"I'll be right here."

The intercom panel reads *Alef, Bet,* and *Gimmel.* My finger stops before the *Bet* button as a little girl screams behind me. A horror movie screech. "Stop it Jonah! Stop, stop." When I turn I see a ten-year-old boy with a fedora on his head, spraying his sister with a water pistol. "I'm telling

Eema, I'm telling Eema," she says, and tears off into the building next door. Sarah's motioning me to push the button. Jonah spins the yellow gun around his finger like Roy Rogers until it flies off and lands on the sidewalk.

"Do you live here?" I ask him.

He points to the gun on the ground and says something in Yiddish.

"Do you speak English?"

The intercom hisses without my touching it. "Is it Chaim?" says a woman's tinny voice.

"Hello?" I say, bowing toward it.

"Chaim?"

"No. No, I'm looking for someone."

"Who?"

"Miriam."

"Are you from the flower shop?"

"No."

"Catering then."

"No. I'm David Arbus. I'm looking for my . . . mother."

In the silence, I try to rehear the woman's voice in my head. It could have been her. I push the button again and there is no response. "Is that you?" I say, my mouth nearly touching the box. "Is that you, Mom?"

Silence.

I step back onto the sidewalk and gaze up at the window. It's impossible to see in her window from here. From the street it's worse, the tree blocks the building to the roof. Maybe I should climb the tree, go through the window?

I move up to press the button again, holding it this time. "Hello? Is Miriam there? Please answer me if it's you. Hello, hello?"

I feel water being squirted on the back of my leg. There's the boy with his gun, standing next to an older, bearded man. "Who are you looking for?" says the man.

I recognize the tiny, slump-shouldered rabbi, the holy man, the one who came to the house so long ago for my mother's *sheitel* ceremony. He has two helpers with him, each holding one of his elbows.

"I'm looking for Miriam," I say.

"Miriam," he says. "I am here for Miriam. She is in apartment *Bet*. Push it. Push the button."

I do, I push it. "Helloooo? It's me again. I'm with other people now," I say into the box.

Silence.

One of the rabbi's helpers tries it. "*Shalom aleichem?* Miriam?" he says. Still no response.

I look back at Sarah and she's pointing at something above and mouthing words I can't hear. I think she's pointing at the tree. I see a branch about five feet from the trunk and so many more, another three feet above it.

"Maybe I can get up there," I say.

"Why would you do that?" says the holy man. "Wait, we'll push it again. She's expecting us."

It takes all my strength to hook my foot on the lowest branch.

"Don't," the rabbi says. "We'll push the button."

I slither my body high enough to get my stomach onto the tree.

"No, no, no," I hear Sarah yell, as my arms slip and I smash my chin on the bark. I jump down with a scrape and look back at Sarah, who's shaking her head.

"Excuse me," I say to the rabbi. "Would you please tell Miriam I was here. I'm her son. Tell her daughter, Dena, that her father is gone, he passed away last week. He was her real father, the father who raised her. And he loved her. His name was Martin Arbus."

"No, no." He is waving his finger now. "What is your name?"

I look back at Sarah, who is still trying to tell me something. "My name is David."

"David. *You* must tell her this," he insists. "You. No one else."

I nod, look into his watery eyes. "I am not a Hasid."

He looks up at the sky, as if to God, and then back to me. "So what?"

When I break into a smile, he does too, and the trillions of wrinkles around his face all splay and deepen.

"Push the button again," he says. "Tell her Rabbi Liebersohn is here to see Dena."

"Dena?"

"Yes. And tell her I don't like to wait."

I step up there again, glancing back at him before pushing it. "Mom?"

Silence.

"Yes?" It's a weak voice, my mother's voice.

"It's your son, David."

"Tomorrow," she says, and I can hear the wobble in her tone. "Today is not a good day."

The rabbi motions for me to push it again.

"Mom?"

"Tomorrow," she says. "Come back tomorrow."

"David!" Sarah yells. She's pointing again, and now I see she's pointing to the window above.

I step back to the sidewalk. My sister. My sister is there. So beautiful, so happy. She laughs at the sight of me, wipes her eyes. "Stay right there!" she says, and disappears from my sight.

Now from the spot where Debra had been, I see my mother, tentative, glancing down at me, tentative but eager.

"Rabbi Liebersohn is here," I say, waving to her. "Come on down. He doesn't like to wait."

DAVID ARBUS
PHOTOGRAPHS
1975–1984
The Portland Museum of Art
Portland, Maine
June 5th–August 30th

ACKNOWLEDGMENTS

I WANT TO THANK my children, Henry and Ella. Thanks for loving me the way you do, and for making me feel so fortunate when I see you each day. Thank you to Mom and Dad and David and Elaine. I am very grateful to all of you. Amy Gash, you're the only editor I'll ever need. Your trust in me made all the difference. Thank you, Amy. Thanks to Sonia Pabley, Elisabeth Scharlatt, Kathleen Caldwell, Debi Echlin, Rabbi Barry Friedman, Stephen and Carol Schulte, Carolyn Hessel, Lynn Carey, Ed Delaney, Jason Headley, Chuck Adams, Laura Girvin, Alexandra Machinist, Adam Braff, Shoshi Braff, Zach Braff, Michelle Braff, Jagger Braff, Lara Brodzinsky, Jessica Kirson, and Jennifer and Peter Gelman.

I love you, Wife.